Frank C Riehl

Poems of the Piasa

Frank C Riehl

Poems of the Piasa

ISBN/EAN: 9783744709545

Printed in Europe, USA, Canada, Australia, Japan

Cover: Foto ©Andreas Hilbeck / pixelio.de

More available books at **www.hansebooks.com**

POEMS OF THE PIASA

BY

FRANK C. RIEHL

———

ALTON, ILL.

MELLING & GASKINS, PUBLISHERS

1896

Unto my mother and my wife,
    Twin hearts of womankind,
In that they have believed in me,
    And never failed to find
Some points of merit in my work:
    With fervency imbibed
In mutual gratitude and love,
    This volume is inscribed.

PREFACE.

OF this little venture into the field of modern literature, appealing to the generosity of the public in general, and of his friends in particular, the author has only to say that it is issued under the advice and at the earnest solicitation of a few persons who believed that the poems contained therein are of sufficient merit to deserve to live, and to have a wider circulation than that afforded by a single publication in the local papers or current magazines.

Of his own thought toward the work, he cannot give better expression than by quoting the following crude lines, which he wrote when a boy of 20 years:

> O, could I but command the words
>   With which to give my feelings wing,
> I'd sing as blithely as the birds
>   Of every fair and noble thing;
> Of all that glads the human soul,
>   And makes life better, I would sing.

I'd sing of friendship, fair and bright,
    Of wayward souls by love redeemed ;
Of countless themes whereon the light
    Of poets' lamp hath never beamed,—
If only I could write the songs
    Which, musing, I have often dreamed.

But no, I never can command
    The words to set my feelings free;
Stern Fate, with her resistless hand,
    Is constantly restraining me,
And I can never be the half
    Of what I fain would wish to be.

Yet is there many a tender strain
    That ne'er escaped the warbler's tongue;
There's many a harp of finest grain
    That ever must remain unstrung,
And many a vision haunts the brain
    Of poets, that shall ne'er be sung.

A boundless gulf must aye remain
    Between the longed-for and the real ;
Earth's feathered songsters strive in vain
    To warble forth the joy they feel;
And every song the poet sings
    Is but the shade of his ideal.

And I will bid my muse sing on,
    Although 'tis but a simple strain ;
Content if, when my life is done,
    And I have left this world of pain,
Some fond soul, pausing at my grave,
    Shall say: "He has not lived in vain."

The poems of Indian legend are given prominent place because they are deemed to be somewhat novel in themselves, and to possess a peculiar local interest in the vicinity of the birth-place of the writer.

The other selections are made from many hundreds of poems, all of which, presented at one reading, might prove an overplus that would pall upon the taste of the kindly disposed and æsthetic patron.

Cordially yours,

THE AUTHOR.

CONTENTS.

INDIAN LAYS AND LEGENDS.

VERSES ON VARIOUS THEMES.

Indian Lays and Legends

SONG OF THE SETTING SUN.

WHILE the sunset glories linger
    On the cloud-hills of the West,
The anthelia's tell-tale finger
    Pointing out each rugged crest,
Let us rest here by the river,
    Where the twilight shadows creep,—
As of old, with bow and quiver,
    Stole the warrior up the steep.

Now the day's reflected glories
    Their soft colorings impart:
As the wit of well-told stories
    Leaves their impress on the heart.
Truly 'tis a charmed surrounding,
    And the very stones we cast,
On the rugged bluffs rebounding,
    Echo the forgotten past,—

Till fond fancy, backward fleeting,
    Paints a picture of the time
When each sun these regions greeting
    Marked the Indian in his prime:
When, his title undisputed,
    He was lord of all he saw,
And his valor, widely bruited,
    Held all rival tribes in awe:

When his pointed arrow speeding
    Faster than the winds are fleet,
Brought the luckless quarry bleeding
    Down within its dark retreat:
While the women, ne'er contending,
    Worked until each task was done,
And the urchins, war pretending,
    Aimed their missiles at the sun.

'T is a vivid presentation,
    Beautiful to look upon,
But it passes, like the nation,
    Into dreamland, and is gone;—
Even as the scenes it cherished,
    Even as the day was fair,
So the memory has perished,
    And the damp of dreath is there.

.Now the fields of maize are growing
    Where the Indian lies at rest,
And the farmer's furrows, flowing,
    Shift the soil above his breast.
Nor shall warrior e'er reviewing
    Here behold the grave's disgrace,
For the stern plowshare of Ruin
    Hath run havoc through the race.

Since they crossed yon peaceful water
    Toward the far Pacific shore,
They have shared the bison's slaughter,
    And pursue the herds no more:
Save the few, who, still remaining,
    By a thankless land ignored,
Their captivity disdaining,
    Choose to perish by the sword.

So this tragedy of nations,
    Like the passing of a day,
Saddest of the world's narrations,
    Marks an epoch passed away;
And the pen that writes the story
    Will have much of good to tell
In the book, of Indian glory,
    Ere the last great chieftain fell.

True, they fought like demons, fired
    With a zeal that stands alone,
Yet their fury was inspired,
    For they did but 'fend their own.
Sparing all equivocation,
    We usurped the red-man's crown
When he spurned civilization,
    By whose sceptre he went down.

Aye, the sun of life is setting
    O'er the Indian's vale of rest,
And the mad world, soon forgetting,
    Surges onward toward the West:
While he waits, with many another,
    When the final trumpet sounds,
To receive his paleface brother
    On the Happy Hunting Grounds.

THE LEGEND OF LOVER'S LEAP.*

SLOW the summer day lies dying, in the
    shadowy arms of night,
And the wind, its requiem sighing, sweeps around
    the headlands white.
Hear it; like a soul in anguish, that, distracted,
    comes to weep,
Fretting its fantastic pinions on the rocks of
    Lover's Leap:
Here, while pale the moonbeams glisten, let us
    sit and muse awhile,
And the prospect will repay us for the moments
    we beguile.

Soft the landscape is, and dreamy, and the stars
    shine overhead:
Far below the rippling waters glide along their
    sandy bed;
Over stream and hill and valley Nature holds her
    court supreme,
And I catch the tender cadence of a golden,
    olden dream.

Sitting here beneath the shelter of the over-
hanging rock,
Comes a Presence stealing o'er me, and it seems
inclined to talk—
To unfold the hidden legend of this point of
Indian fame,
All the strange, unwritten story how it came to
bear its name.

Long ago, so runs the record, ere the paleface
saw the land,
And the red man in his glory trod the river's
shining sand,
Came a maiden here to worship every evening,
when the sun
Dipped behind the Western woodland, and the
daily chase was done—
Came to thank the Blessed Spirit for the many
mercies sent,
And to ask for all her people grace and plenty,
and content.

Fair she was, this dusky damsel, daughter of the
tribal chief,
And she bore a charmed existence in the popular
belief:

Many of the brave young warriors had contended
    for her hand,
And though all had failed to win her, all were
    slaves to her command.

But it chanced one fatal evening, gazing hence
    across the stream,
She beheld a youthful boatman in the early
    twilight gleam,
And she hailed the comely stranger, till he
    turned in at the shore:
He was of another people, whom she ne'er had
    known before.
Each found pleasure in the other, and the chance
    acquaintance grew
Till they vowed to bide together, and exchanged
    love's pledges true.
But, alas! one eve they lingered, gazing on the
    peaceful tide,
As the youth told his devotion, kneeling fondly
    by her side,
When their tryst was rudely broken, through a
    jealous rival's eyes
Who beheld an interloper winning thus his
    cherished prize,

And at once did spread the story that a hated
      enemy
Was enticing their fair princess from her native
      tribe to flee.

Then the chieftain, flushed with anger, siezed
      his trusty bow and dart,
And forbade his warriors weapons—he would
      pierce the villain's heart:
Stealthily he stole upon them, all unconscious of
      their doom,
Till his shout of warning echoed like a death-
      knell through the gloom;
Instantly the maiden, pleading, sprang to shield
      her lover's form;
Woe! the deadly arrow speeding, sought her life-
      blood, fresh and warm:
Then the grim old warrior staggered,—he, a
      master in his art,
Who had never missed a target, shot his
      daughter through the heart;
And the youth, when comprehending, caught the
      fair form in his arms
While the angry horde, advancing, pressed him
      close with wild alarms;

When he sprang upon yon boulder, stood a
    moment calmly there,
Cast at them a cold defiance—then leaped out
    upon the air.

Afterwards they found them, mangled, lying on
    the rocks below,
And the hills re-echoed, sadly, the remorseful
    cries of woe.
Tenderly the twain were buried, on the summit,
    side by side,
While the Indian priest, foreknowing, at the
    service prophesied
That the place should e'er be sacred to the
    spirit it had served,
As the home of many people who these favors
    well deserved—
That the Manitou's best blessings, ever coming
    from above,
Here would hold his chosen children in the
    happy bonds of love.

* * *

Little dreamed the savage savant how his words
    would be fulfilled,
That another, conquering nation on this sacred
    spot would build,

When his own had crossed the river, driven,
  never to return,
To the distant, arid regions where the sunset
  glories burn:—
Little recked he of the changes, coming down the
  vales of Time,
That should blight his native woodlands in the
  grandeur of their prime,
When a wilderness of wigwams, mountain high
  beside his own,
Should obliterate his footprints from the land
  which he had known.
But he spoke with truth inspired: Though the
  Indian's sun hath set,
And his memory, most forgotten, only lingers
  with us yet
In a score of doubtful legends, such as that
  rehearsed above;
Illustrative of his nature, passionate with hate
  and love:—
Other hearts here oft have spoken loves as true
  as theirs of old,
And exchanged some tender token as the fateful
  tale was told:

And we hold the place in rev'rence, as each
 ⌐ passing season brings
Joys that bide in every household, like a dove
    with folded wings,
While the voice of new endeavor, ever just before
    us, leads
On to braver, worthier efforts, loftier aims and
    better deeds.
Yes, methinks I have been dreaming, and we,
    too, must go to rest,
For the morrow brings new duties and another,
    nobler quest:
Peace enwraps the slumbering city, but the winds
    their vigils keep
Crooning their prophetic murmurs round the point
    of Lover's Leap.

OUATOGA.*

BRAVE Chieftain of that honored tribe
    Of Red Men, who presided o'er
These fertile regions of the West,
    By mighty Mississippi's shore:
We owe thee much of gratitude
    Who gavest the name of Illini
A deathless honor, facing death
    As one who does not fear to die
When duty calls. 'Twas thine to make
    The noblest conquest life may know,
Of sacrifice for others sake,
    When evil shadows hover low.
A savage king of savage land,
    'Twas by creation's highest law
That thou wast nerved to raise thy hand
    Against the monster, Piasa.
Thou and thy warriors little kenned
    That, in the course of years to be,
Another nation would commend
    The deed that set thy people free.
Thine was the impulse; ours the meed
    Of profit, in the fruit it gave,
Through that fair flower of val'rous deed
    That blossoms o'er thy nameless grave.

THE WARRIOR'S LAMENT.

FROWNING stood the grizzled [grayish] chieftain on the
desecrated mound,
Gazing like a wounded eagle on the fertile fields
around;
Stern and sad, his brows were furrowed with the
seams [scars] of many woes,
And his waving locks were whitened by the fall
of countless snows.
Silently he gazed about him, over all the varied
scene—
Saw the waving fields and orchards and the
roads that wound between:
Marked the sites of happy homesteads, studding
all the rolling plain,
And across his clouded visage [face] came a look of
stifled pain.

21

"O, Great Spirit of my fathers," thus at last
    his thought found breath,
"Who for many years have slumbered in this
    mound the sleep of death,
Why, when you laid down the hatchet on the
    battlefield of life,
Did you leave your luckless children to keep up
    the bitter strife?
Ah, my mother, you who bore me, when those
    bones were laid to rest,
Why was I not buried with you, locked in
    slumber on your breast?
Better to have died in childhood, better have
    remained unborn,
Then have lived to see my people made to bear
    the white man's scorn!
O, great Father, mighty river, when we crossed
    yon silver tide
Little thought we of the sorrows which that fatal
    step implied!
Banished from our native forests, driven from our
    fathers' graves,
We were promised peace and plenty 'yond the
    Mississippi's waves;

Thus we went away, in sadness, left our
        heritage behind,
On the far-off Western prairies other hunting
        grounds to find.
Did the pale-face keep his promise? No, for
        scarcely had we gone
When his armies, coming after, forced my people
        to move on!
Onward still the white man's powder drives us
        toward the setting sun,
And will never cease to urge us till the fatal race
        is run:
Westward yet across the mountains is the Indian
        forced to flee
And ere long his race must perish, 'whelmed
        beneath the rolling sea.
Blame us not, Eternal Spirit, that we should
        resist so long—
That we rise again in protest to resent this
        mighty wrong.

"Once again the gray-haired warrior stands
        beside the tribal grave,
'Mid the maze of desolation, by his native river's
        wave:

Could an Indian's curses blight them, in their
    arrogance and pride,
I would lay these fields in ruin, scatter all their
    homesteads wide!
Not the gauntlet of the death-dance and the torture
    at the stake,
Not the Indian's darkest vengeance could enough
    atonement make
For the wrongs which he has suffered at the
    spoiler's ruthless hand,
Who now rules in proud dominion in my people's
    native land.
But 'tis vain, my race is fallen, and can never
    rise again
Till the Manitou shall call us to the happy
    regions. Then,
When the Indian and the pale-face stand before
    him in the throng,
He will hold his mighty council and decide which
    one was wrong.
Farewell, Spirit of my Fathers, for the time is
    growing late,
I must go to join my people, and to share their
    final fate.''

Yet he stood awhile in silence, as if fettered by
a spell,
Stooping then to earth he kissed it: thus he took
his last farewell.
Then he wrapped his cloak about him and in
silence strode away,—
Off, toward the sunset regions, passing with the
dying day.

THE CROSSING OF THE SIOUX.*

PORTAGE des Sioux, historic place,
　　Nestled beside the peaceful shore,
An unpretentious village now,
　　But rich in legendary lore,—
Where plods the busy throng to-day,
　　And from yon lofty steeple side
The chimes that call to evening prayer
　　Float o'er the restful river's tide—
Where sings the farmer as he guides
　　His plowshare through the mellow soil,
. And bounteous harvests every year
　　Reward him well for honest toil.

Time was when all was wild and drear
　　Within the dark, primeval wood,
Save here and there, where on the ridge
　　A straggling group of wigwams stood.

Here reigned the red man all supreme,
  Plied undisturbed the huntsman's art,
Nor owned a foe more brave than he
  Who dared to cross his deadly dart.
The battle cry, the fleeting chase,
  Roused all his passions, all his joy;
And many a haughty challenge met
  The neighboring tribes of Illinois.

And once, so runs the legend old,
  There came a panic to the land:
A foe so terrible to meet,
  The bravest did not dare withstand.
Small tribal feuds were soon forgot
  In the dread fate which threatened all,
The strongest turned his back and fled
  Before the awful monster's call.
Then came, howe'er, a day of joy
  When every warrior, child and squaw,
In savage exultation danced
  About the slaughtered Piasa.

Where towers yon holy temple now,
  Marquette—the earliest white man—trod,
And standing 'midst the pagan throng
  First taught them of the Christian's God.

'Twas later yet by many moons
  When that historic struggle came
Which brought about the strategy
  Wherefrom the village has its name.
Two nations ruled these lowland plains,
  The wily Sioux and fiery Crow
And ne'er two feudal warriors met
  But flint was sped from bended bow.

Thus once a scouting band of Sioux
  Ventured too far on foreign soil,
Nor ever thought of danger till
  Encircled by the foeman's toil.
But with a quick, decisive move
  The Sioux broke through the attacking rank,
Seizing a score of staunch canoes
  Moored close beside the sandy bank;
Then down the dark Missouri's flood
  A race of life and death began,
Two scores of fugitives pursued
  By hosts—a score to every man.

Wild is the flight; with deafening yells
  The Crows come surging down the stream;
Like lances glinting in the sun
  Their paddles o'er the waters gleam:

And six good throws below, the Sioux
    With features set in sullen pride,
Bend every muscle to the strokes,
    As through the rushing waves they glide.
With courage fostered of despair
    They forge ahead and surely gain;
But still the murderous host comes on
    While flint-capped arrows fall like rain.

For hours the maddening contest lasts,
    The strongest failing, faint and sore,
When suddenly, around a bend,
    They vanish and are seen no more.
Just where, almost, the rivers meet,
    When, veering sharply in its flow,
The mad Missouri turns to join
    The Mississippi miles below,
With practiced eye the Sioux perceived
    A chance to 'scape the victim's doom:
Landed, and carrying their canoes,
    Quick vanished in the forest gloom.

Brief was the march, and soon they found
    Them by their native river's waves,
Re-launched, and paddled safely back
    To join their squaws and fellow braves.

The Crows, not 'ware that aught was wrong,
    Kept madly on their fruitless course,
And were in turn pursued, engaged,
    And routed by superior force.

* * *

Thus did the village find its name;
    The race that since hath settled here,
Descendants of De Soto's men—
    Still hold the legend fondly dear.
Ask any burgher you may meet;
    He will avow the story true,
And point that narrow neck of land
    That marks the crossing of the Sioux.

ILLIOLA'S. PENANCE.*

WALKING down the peaceful valley, 'neath
the silvery summer moon,
To the spring whose crystal waters gurgle forth,
a precious boon,
From the hills whose rock-ribbed contour cir-
cumscribes the starry sky,
Comes to me a dreamful story, whence I know
not, neither why,—
Comes as from the sparkling fountain, through
the music of its flow,
In an idyl of devotion from the days of long ago.

Dwelt there once an Indian Princess yonder by
the river side,
Graced with Nature's richest favors, and a boon
of tender pride
In the wigwam of her people, who esteemed her
half divine, .
As the Manitou had sent her to achieve some
great design.

Frail of form, yet fair and graceful as the fern
  leaves at her feet;
True and tender and devoted, and of bearing
  rarely sweet;
Guileless as the dappled deerling, brought her
  when the hunt was done:
Winsome as the woodland roses smiling at the
  morning sun:—
Was the Princess Illiola, daughter of the reigning
  chief,
On the eve of her great sorrow, in the gloomy
  vale of grief.

Never womanhood so perfect lived of manhood
  unadmired,
And the hope to gain her favor many daring
  deeds inspired
In the warriors of her people, who were never
  loth to go
To the chase, or e'en to battle, with an un-
  relenting foe.
Of the many, two were favored by her fond
  approving eye;
Both were counted brave and manly, and no arm
  with theirs could vie;

Each adored the peerless maiden, and their
     trophies, one by one,
Graced the entrance to her wigwam when the
     daily hunt was done:
Brothers were they in relation, twin of birth and
     one of mind,
But she vowed the love to neither that to either
     was inclined.

Came a day of autumn glory, when the Princess
     walked alone,
Aimlessly about the valley, wrapped in musings
     all her own;
Thinking of the ardent lovers—maybe searching
     in her heart
Whom to give the wifely favor, whom to send
     the cruel dart,
For she felt in sense of duty that the time to act
     was near,
And—the sound of angry voices broke upon her
     startled ear:
'Twas the brothers hot in parley; and she stole
     with noiseless tread
Till she heard, in trembling terror, all the bitter
     things they said,

Standing there in grim defiance. It was Illiola's
    name
That had drowned all thought of kinship in a
    flood of savage flame.
They had slain an antlered monarch; each had
    hunted unaware
Of the other's like endeavor, each had aimed his
    missile fair,
And· each claimed the noble quarry, vowed the
    conquest all his own
For a gift to Illiola. Woe! Upon that bed of
    stone
Fell two forms athwart the carcass, and an arrow
    in each breast
Told the 'wildered, weeping maiden what her
    heart had never guessed.

When they found her on the morrow, reason's
    light had left her eyes,
And the soul of Illiola moaned its requiem to the
    skies.
All the sages of the nation came to minister, in
    vain,
To the Chieftain's beauteous daughter; none
    could ease the fatal pain;

Like a broken flower she faded, pining by the
    valley-side
Where the tragedy transpired, and, with the new
    moon, she died.

But that night there came a Presence, and her
    people heard a voice,
Softer than the sound of waters, and it counseled
    thus: "Rejoice!
Do not weep for Illiola, for the Manitou hath said
That her spirit, here abiding, shall redeem the
    life-blood shed,
In a consecrated fountain; washing out the
    crimson stain
Of the lover's last encounter, to the nation's
    lasting gain.
Here shall sorrows be requited, while the ill find
    health anew,
And all jealous passions mingle in a better,
    broader view,
When the people meet to counsel, in the dawn
    of brighter day,
As yon stains by these bright waters are suffused
    and washed away.''

Looking, they beheld the wonder of the boulder
     rent apart,
And from out the fissured crevice saw the
     sparkling water start;
Stooped the Chief, and quaffing deeply, spoke:
     "The Manitou·be praised;
Be this valley consecrated to His service," and
     he raised
In his hands a shining pebble, and concluded,
     calm and clear:
"So may Illiola's penance brighten all who tarry
     here."

* * *

Hath it seemed a Pagan story? Here we are
     beside the spring;
Drink we to the spirit maiden, while the service
     vespers ring,
And the words of counsel falling from the
     platform seneschal,
Seem to echo Illiola's benediction over all.

ON A PICTURE OF SITTING BULL.

GRIM warrior, as we gaze upon
    The painted likeness of thy face,
How sadly we recall with thee
    The story of thy ill-starred race.
Resistless will and manly power
    Are on those features interlined,
And stamped upon that lofty brow
    The impress of a haughty mind.

The last and greatest of the line
    Of fighting chiefs,—majestic, brave;
We honor thee despite thy deeds;
    And oft beside that lonely grave
The patriot in awe will pause,
Remembering thee and thy lost cause.

RICHARDVILLE.*

BESIDE St. Mary's silver stream,
    Whose laughing waters, all agleam,
Flow past the city of Fort Wayne,
Through Indiana's fertile plain,
There stands within a churchyard gray—
Long since surrendered to decay—
A weather-beaten shaft of stone,
With moss and lichens overgrown,
Upon whose surface may be traced
These words, by time almost effaced:

"Here rest the bones of Richardville,
    Great chief of the Miami tribe.
An Indian statesman of great skill,
    Who never gave nor took a bribe."

The story of the warrior's name,
Although, perchance, unknown to fame,
Is still remembered and revered
Upon the plains where he was reared,

And honored as among the few
Red men who upright were, and true.
Though now his race has passed away,
And scarcely in this latter day
Do we take trouble to recall
The hated people from whose fall
We date our own prosperity,
Yet in this chieftain's life we see
Enough of nobleness to prove
That one, at least, could feel and love.

Full ten-score years ago, and more,
When on St. Mary's wooded shore
The swarthy Indian proudly stood,
Unchallenged monarch of the wood;
When first the white man dared to brave
The wilds beyond Ohio's wave,
And many a hero lost his life
Upon the stake or by the knife,
One day the tribe, in council grave,
Met by the peaceful river's wave.
Some, boasting, showed their battle scars,
While others plotted future wars;
From wigwams swaying in the breeze
Blue smoke curled upward through the trees,

Within, the dusky squaws were bent,
Each on some toilsome task intent,
And on the stream to instinct true
The urchin plied his fleet canoe,
Or launched into a tree the dart
That should have pierced a foeman's heart;
Thus grouped the savage host, serene,
Encamped upon the peaceful scene.
But this was not the business yet
For which the braves that day were met;
'Twas matter of a darker dye
That spoke in every warrior's eye.

Near by, though from the throng away,
There stood a squaw with locks of gray,
And standing by her side a youth
Whose eye betrayed a heart of truth,
A soul with wild ambition fired,
A mind of lofty thoughts inspired,
His every look and act confessed
A nobler lineage than the rest,
Gathered within the camp that day
To while the loitering hours away.
The woman was the widowed dame
Of him, now gone, whose peerless name

Honored by all the tribe had stood
Supreme, as patriarch of the wood.
Her fondest hope and single prayer
   Was that she might survive the hour
To see the lad beside her there
   Invested with his father's power.

   But valor was the only rod
By which these warriors would be ruled,
In danger's front had they been schooled,
   And they would brook no other god.
Thus, though they owned the stripling's blood,
And mourned his mother's widowhood,
Those heroes of a hundred wars—
Deep seamed by honored battle scars—
Would never bow beneath his will
Until, by some brave act of skill,
Or master deed he should evince
The prowess of an Indian prince.
Hence was the tribe together come
To choose, from out their number, one
To lead their wars and councils sage
Till their young chief should come of age.

But hark! Above the lazy breeze
That whispered soft among the trees
Was heard the sound of many feet,
As through the forest's still retreat
A party came with hurried tramp,
Dragging a prisoner into camp.
With hands and feet securely bound,
The captive sank upon the ground.
A son of that despised race!
Reflected on that manly face
The resignation of despair:
For well he knew no friends were there
To save him from that awful fate—
The savage zeal to satiate.

Past was the time of lethargy;
All danced about in ghoulish glee,
Anticipating soon to see
Their victim writhing at the stake,
Which awful rite alone could slake
The vengeance of the Indian's heart.
Briefly the braves communed apart,
Not long, for in each mind foredoomed,
The verdict was: "To be consumed
By torture at the burning stake."
So spake they all; none there to take

The pale-face' part. The dread decree,
Announced, was hailed with wildest glee.
Some hastened to prepare the tree,
While others for the fagots went
In frenzied zeal; each soul was bent
On hastening the fearful rite.
The captive, lying pale and white,
Heroically endured the taunts,
The cruel blows and savage vaunts,
Cast upon him from every side.
At last he stood, securely tied;
All was prepared; the lighted brand
Blazed in the iron warrior's hand.

"Now go, my son, and do thy part!"
Cried she who all the while apart
Beside the youth in silence stood:
"Now go and prove thy sire's blood
Runs not for nothing in thy veins.
Quick! or too late will be thy pains!"
Then suddenly the flames leaped out,
As round the pile with deafening shout,
The awful dance of death began,
When, lo! across the circle ran,
Resistless as a thunder storm,
With lightning speed, a slender form,

Scattered like reeds the crackling brands,
Released the prisoner's feet and hands,
And, placing in his grasp the knife,
Bade him be gone and fly for life.
Then, turning to the astonished band,
He shouted, with uplifted hand:

"If you must kill, then murder me,
But let this hapless man go free!
My sire's blood is in these veins,
And well ye know his soul disdained
Thus cowardly to take the life
Of one with whom he had no strife."

Half stupefied, the warriors gazed
Upon the youth, and saw, amazed,
Him who had dared this brave relief,
The son of their departed chief.
The flash of anger in their eyes
Gave place to looks of deep surprise:
Then admiration for his deed
Secured for him the highest meed
Which a brave warrior could receive.
Thus what began an awful rite,
Ended a feast of proud delight;
Each warrior in that swarthy band

Advanced to kiss the stripling's hand,
And owned him ruler of the land.

Long lived the youth, a ruler brave,
Beside St. Mary's peaceful wave.
He drew his bow in many a fight,
But ever on the side of right,
And through his life, until the end,
He still remained the white man's friend.
In battle strong, in council skilled,
He won the name of Richardville,
And over Indiana's plains,
Where erst this noble savage reigned,
His name is known and honored still.

In after years, when wars had ceased,
While signing documents of peace,
He met the man whose life was saved
When first his people's wrath he braved.
Each clasped the other as a friend,
And so remained until the end.
The debt of life was well repaid,
And when the chieftain's bones were laid
To rest beside their native stream,
The other, showing his esteem,

Raised o'er his grave this shaft of stone,
And carved the lines you see thereon:

"Pilgrim, when idly passing here,
  Tread lightly o'er this sacred mound,
And grudge it not one manly tear,
  For know, you tread on sainted ground."

A DUEL ON THE PLAINS.

NUNECHI and Swapi were warriors as brave
    As ever encountered an enemy's glave,
And oft through the Nation, when ranges were
    wide,
They chased the fleet quarry, or fought side by
    side;
Each man was endowed with the gift of his
    race,—
Great physical powers and sinewy grace,—
Both highly esteemed in the great tribal creed,
That dare-devil courage is valor, indeed,
And each held the other in highest regard,
As worthy an Indian's most cherished reward.

But one sorry day when their passions were fired
They changed to the likeness of demons inspired.
'Twas at the wild race-meet, where each tribal
    steed
Was run o'er the courses for mettle and speed,
There, first in the saddle and last in the field,
These twain were victorious, but neither would
    yield

The other his laurels, till, breaking at last,
The steeds interfered,—and the challenge was
    cast.
Impulsively savage, their passions once crossed,
The friendship of years in an instant was lost,
And, glaring defiance, each in the same breath
Demanded the right of a fight to the death.

Friends, half comprehending, looked on in dismay,
But in the dread finale had little to say,
For deep in the heart of the Indian is set
The maxim to never forgive or forget,
And having inflicted the greatest offense
Their customs afforded, through hatred intense,
Each bystander knew that to protest were vain,
Since only their life-blood could wipe out the
    stain.
Hence sadly the old chieftain gave his consent,
And straight the two warriors, on murder intent,
Selected their seconds, the surest of shot,
And armed them as guards of the dueling spot;
When, clasping a glittering knife in each hand,
They entered the circle and took their last stand.

In all the vast concourse no murmur was heard,
The contestants, glaring, exchanged not a word,

Forgetting the onlookers standing inert,
Each nerve at full tension, each fibre alert.
They stood as the panther preparing to spring,
Then cautiously crossed and recrossed in the
    ring.
Each felt that his uttermost skill would be tried,
And knew what a single false movement implied.
Look! quick as the lightning each turns on his
    heel,
And naught save the flashing and clashing of
    steel
Is marked for a moment, then, breaking, they
    part,
With neither a scratch,—what a marvel of art!
But quick as a flash they return to the fray,
And now there is blood, and Nunechi gives way;
No! see, 'tis a feint; aye! and Swapi goes down,
But not for Nunechi the conqueror's crown;
For e'en as he bends the last blow to impart,
He falls and expires with a knife in his heart.
Now hail they the champion, whose conquering
    yell
Defies the poor clay of the warrior who fell;
But see how he falters, how lowers his head!
He falls, and both victor and vanquished are
    dead.

PAWNADAWA'S VENGEANCE.*

ON the shore of Lake Superior, one eventful
afternoon,—
'Twas a quiet summer's evening in the pleasânt
month of June—
Stood a scornful Indian beauty, fondly dreaming,
half awake,
Idly gazing at the shadows on the bosom of the
lake,—
Stood the winsome Pawnadawa, lost in medita-
tion sweet,
Thinking of the pale-face lover whom she waited
there to meet.

Nature had bestowed upon her symmetry of form
and face,
Graces that were seldom granted to the daughters
of her race;

*Note VII.—Appendix.

Yes, she was indeed a beauty, as she stood
     serenely there,
Playfully the evening breezes tossed about her
     raven hair,
While, commingled with her tresses was a veri-
     colored wreath,
And her pouting lips, half parted, showed two
     rows of pearly teeth.

Yet her bearing condescending showed a pride
     that made her vain,
And she looked upon her sisters of the camp with
     cold disdain;
Many times had she been courted by the gallants
     of her tribe,
Many braves from other nations came to woo
     with costly bribe,
But no words or wiles could win her, and she
     sent each one away
To be mocked by luckless rivals, who had seen
     their humble day.

For the shaft had not been feathered that should
     pierce her wanton heart,
Till the stranger from the city came to woo with
     practiced art,

As a special trusted agent for the traders in the
     East,
Giving for their furs munitions and provisions
     for the feast.
Dwelt he as a prince among them, far removed
     from home and friends,
And the kindred social joys whereon so much of
     life depends.

Sought he oft her father's wigwam, coming as an
     honored guest,
Where he saw the little maiden, ever bright and
     self-possessed,   .
Till he came almost to love the sportive, way-
     ward forest child;
Many happy, fleeting hours in her presence he
     beguiled,
And resolved at last to woo her to submission, if
     he could;
She would make a sweet companion for him in
     this lonely wood.

When the time should come for leaving, and his
     mission here was o'er,
He could leave her with her people—oft had this
     been done before,

So he flattered and caressed her, pressed his suit
  with presents gay,
Told her fancy-colored stories of his people, far
  away,—
Told the tale of Pocahontas, and the homage she
  received
From the lofty lords and ladies in the land beyond
  the seas:

Told her that the pale-face maidens, spite of all
  their wordly goods,
Could they see her, all would envy his dear
  princess of the woods.
Thus with cajoleries and falsehoods he aroused
  her love and pride
Till he knew that he had won her,—that she fain
  would be his bride.
Thus we find her by the lakeside on this summer's evening fair,
Waiting for the fair deceiver who had vowed to
  to meet her there.

Hist! she must have heard him coming, for a
  smile is on her lips,
And as lightly as a feather to her bark near by
  she skips,

When, with burst of merry laughter, quick she
    glides out from the shore,
Leaves him standing disconcerted, though reluc-
    tant to implore.
"Ha, my Ernest is a sluggard; you have kept
    me waiting long,
And I've half a mind to leave you here, to suffer
    for my wrong."

"O, my Bright Eyes, do not leave me, come;
    see here what I have got."
And her eyes beheld the present; further words
    he needed not.
She returned, received the trinket, and repaid
    him with a kiss,
So the twain embarked together in an ecstacy of
    bliss;
When she headed for an island, gaily laughing,
    full of glee,
And went skipping o'er the water like a gull·
    upon the sea.

There the fatal farce was acted; there, before
    the twilight came,
He had asked the maid to wed him, she had
    vowed to bear his name.

Ah! If on that fateful evening then he thought
    he held his prize,
He had seen the fiends of passion hid beneath
    those laughing eyes!
Could he then have known her truly, quickly
    had he changed his mind,
But the soul of man is willful, and a lover
    always blind.

He had with him an assistant who was better
    versed than he
In the book of Indian nature, and it pained his
    heart to see,
This young, self-deluded lover rushing onward to
    his fate,
Yet he had not dared to caution, till, alas! it
    was too late.
But that night he was returning from a hunt
    along the strand,
And beheld the tender parting of the twain upon
    the sand;

Heard the fulsome words they uttered, saw their
    kisses fondly blend,
And resolved to wait no longer, but at once to
    warn his friend.

Hence that evening, after supper, as he laid
     aside his pan,
He sat down beside his messmate, cleared his
     throat and thus began:
"I'm afraid you are in danger from an unsus-
     pected foe,
Would you mind if I should tell you?" "Heavens,
     no, what is it, Joe?"

"Do you mean to wed that maiden?" "Does it
     matter if I do?"
"Not to me," Joe answered, dryly, "but, my
     boy, it does to you;
Take my warning, if you wed her, you will rue
     it ere you part,
Better try to tame a serpent than that little
     witch's heart."
"Gracious! man, what makes you think so?"
     asked Lefare with wounded pride;
"What would make me think of otters if I came
     across their slide?

"I have roamed these woods too often with the
     rifle and the axe,
And have seen too many varmints not to know
     them by their tracks;

I have spent my life among them—and my hair
      is turning gray—
Yet I never met a creature half as treacherous as
      they."
"No, Joe, you are much mistaken, she is deep
      in love with me."
"Well, perhaps she is at present, but this will
      not always be.

"Do you mean to take her with you when this
      trading business ends?"
"Take a copper-colored wife home, to be
      laughed at by my friends?
Heavens, man, you must be crazy: I shall leave
      her here, of course—
Here, among these savage people there's no ban
      upon divorce."
"Well, then, wed her if you want to, but
      remember what I say,
Better watch the vixen's motions, or you'll come
      to grief some day.

"You had rather quit this business and—great
      gophers! what was that?"
"Nothing but a startled otter, or a frightened
      water rat."

Yes, an otter; had he seen her, crawling by the
water's edge,
Every fibre of her being quivering with stifled
rage!
She had listened to their council, overheard the
whole debate,
And her passion in a moment turned from love to
burning hate.

Ah! If e'er the King of Evil sat enthroned on
human brow,
He was undisputed master of the Indian beauty
now.
On she flew, her headlong passions broken loose
from all control,
Raging like a band of furies through the chambers
of her soul.
Yet she met him on the morrow with a lover's
gentle zest,
And no sign betrayed the tempest that was
raging in her breast.

Till he questioned, all unconscious of the maiden's
fell design:
"O my Bright Eyes, little darling, tell me when
you will be mine?"

"At the foot of yonder boulder, if to-morrow
   morn be fair,
There will Bright Eyes come to meet thee; go
   and wait thy answer there."
Gladly he obeyed her summons, in the morning
   fair and clear,
He sat waiting by the tryst-place for the maiden
   to appear.

Long he lingered, till the sunshine, rising clear
   above the hills,
Kissed the dew from off the grasses, dried the
   mists above the rills,
Yet he did not see her coming; what could make
   her stay so late?
Surely something had detained her. He determined yet to wait.
Then he heard a sound behind him, turned, and
   with a shudder sprang
As a rattlesnake that moment, hissing, struck
   with gaping fang,

Then another and another: from all sides he saw
   them come,
Wakened by their leader's challenge, and he
   stood with terror dumb,

When a shout of ringing laughter grated harshly
      on his ear:—
"O, my Bright Eyes! help me! save me!" cried
      he, almost crazed with fear;
"Ha! Lefare!—thy tongue is falser than the ser-
      pents at thy feet,
But I am the only maiden whom its lies will
      ever cheat.

"On that same accursed evening when I promised
      to be thine,
I was close beside thy wigwam, overheard thy
      fell design;
Made a wife and then deserted for another? We
      shall see;
Here I bade thee seek thy answer, fiery tongues
      will give it thee."
"If you have a woman's pity," cried he, almost
      choked for breath,
"If you have a heart within you, save me from
      this awful death."

But the venom touched his vitals, and he leaped
      in air and fell;
Then she watched them pile upon him like a
      thousand fiends of hell,—

Saw him fight like one enchanted, with the
      courage of despair,
While the reptiles coiled about him, mingled with
      his flowing hair;
And at last when all was ended, and the tortured
      soul was gone,
Still she stood there, high above them, shouting
      loud to hiss them on.

Then she sought old Joe, the trapper; with a
      laugh no tongue could mock,
"Go," she said, "thy master waits thee at the
      base of yonder rock."
O, the agonies that filled him when he saw that
      awful sight,
Others might have been deluded, but he judged
      the scene aright.
He secured the mangled body from the vengeance
      of the snakes,
And with tender care interred it in a vale beside
      the lake.

Even then he saw the woman, still unsatisfied,
      he thought,
Laughing like some fiend incarnate at the havoc
      she had wrought.

"God forgive me," said the veteran, in an
        agony of strife,
"It is very wrong I know for man to take a
        human life—
But,"—the ringing of a rifle cut the final sen-
        tence short,
And the soul of Pawnadawa took its flight with
        the report.

Quickly, then, he hurried forward, saw the Indian
        girl was dead,
And, beset with sudden terror, leaped in his
        canoe and fled.
Judge not harshly, gentle reader, 'twas a murder
        to be sure,
But a man is only mortal—there are things he
        can't endure.

PASSING OF THE MONARCH.*

SILENCE deep, and keenest sorrow, shroud the
     valley like a pall,
While the news, in whispers broken, casts a
     death-damp over all.
Rolls the mighty Mississippi past the wigwam at
     the feet
Of the braves, so late victorious, abject now, in
     dumb retreat:
And the very heart of Nature seems to ache with
     stifled pain,
For that life-chord, rudely broken, fondly cher-
     ished, mourned in vain.

He is gone, the brave and noble, child of Nature,
     master-man,
Chief by right of native merit, crowned and
     honored by the clan;

*Note VIII.—Appendix.   63

Peerless in the field of action, strong and stead-
fast, sure of aim;
In the council fair and fearless, true to every
fireside claim.
Fell with him his royal station, there is none to
fill his place:
Though his life's interpretation lingers, like a
parting grace.

In the river's grasp they found him, where, full
robed, he sank to sleep;
While the birds forgot their carols, and the skies
above did weep:
Yet we know, could he have willed it, he had
chosen so to die,
And each mortal course is ordered by the Manitou on high.
Soft in mother earth they laid him, far beyond
the rolling wave,
And the winds of passing seasons sigh their
requiems o'er his grave.

"PILOT'S GUIDE."*

"CAPTAIN," queried my companion—we were
    speeding with the stream,
In the early summer twilight, as it were a
    pleasant dream,
Just below old Hamburg city, steaming toward
    the Illinois,
Where it meets the Mississippi, and the steamer's
    graceful poise,
As she glided o'er the waters like a thing of
    conscious pride,
Formed an interesting contrast to the scene on
    either side:—
"Captain, yonder on the hill-top, towering lofty
    and alone,
I perceive a strange white object, like a chiseled
    shaft of stone:

---

*Note IX.—Appendix,

Am I right in the conjecture that it represents
    some mark
Of historical occurrence—of some depredation dark
Wrought by gory-handed Indians on the sturdy
    pioneers,
Who sought here to found their homesteads in
    the nation's early years?"

"Well, no," said the Captain slowly, stepping
    to the larboard side,
"That old monument up yonder is the river
    pilot's guide,
And no Indian as I know of caused it to be
    planted there,
Though the redskins once were plenty in these
    regions everywhere.
Over there they fought their battles, on that
    desolated plain,
And they say that one whole nation in a single
    fight was slain;
People go there every season in the grass to
    search around,
And some very ugly weapons have been taken
    from the ground.

Over here the dead were buried, and these bluffs
     are lined with graves,
Where repose the crumbling frames of many
     hundred fallen braves;
Scientists oft come to dig them from beneath
     the covering stones,
And have sometimes found old arrows sticking in
     the brittle bones.

"But excuse me, sir; you asked about the story
     of the shaft
Standing on yon crowning hill-top, which we are
     just leaving aft. ·
You have read of Enoch Arden? Well, sir, this
     was such a man,
Only no one ever found out where his troubled
     life began.
And he never told his secret; he was here before
     we came,
Yes, a pioneer of pilots, Marvin Thomas was his
     name.
He came with the early traffic on this noble
     inland stream,
Of the first to stem its current by the agency
     of steam.

Many years he plied these waters, and sometime
 the boys still feel
As if Thomas were beside them, with his hand
 upon the wheel;
He was liked by all who knew him, though he
 never sought a friend,
Always ready, on occasion, with a helping hand
 to lend.

"Thus he lived and died among us; but before
 he passed away,
Made us take his little savings, hoarded for a
 rainy day,
And exacted solemn promise that his clay should
 be interred
On that hillside, where the murmur of the waters
 can be heard
In their tender, mournful cadence, whose refrain
 shall never cease,—
That he might lie down contented, and his spirit
 rest in peace.
So we buried him up yonder, and that monument
 was raised
In remembrance of him and of the early boating
 days.

And whenever we are passing, any time of day
      or night,
Every eye in that direction seems to turn with
      keen delight;
Like a sentinel on duty, high above the river's
      tide,
It fulfills its friendly mission, and we call it
      'Pilots' Guide.' "

Verses on Various Themes

THE FOIL OF FATE.*

HARK, ye who have listened to stories of old,
From history's pages and narratives told,
Of mortal encounters on honor's grim field,
Where blood paid the ransom that pride would
not yield:
Not oft in the book of American fame
Do such things reflect on the nation's fair name;
But once, eight and forty long summers ago,
Where yon river's waters so placidly flow,
There crossed out of Alton a boat-load of men,
Intent on a conflict as thrilling as when
Burr pointed his pistol with well-practiced art,
And sent a ball crashing through Hamilton's heart.

The flower and pride of the young Prairie State—
The veterans of finance and peers of debate—
Were parties to that dread excursion, whose end
Each dreading, fore-guessed in the death of his
friend—

Or one or the other of two men, whose life
Was linked with the issues of national strife;
Each young in the vigor of manhood and deeds,
Espousing the tenets of opposite creeds;
Each standing for principles equally strong,
Inspired by the lilt of ambition's glad song,
Though holding already high places of trust
In office and council. They came to adjust
A personal question of honor so grave
That nothing, they deemed, short of bloodshed
        could save
The fair name of either; and yet was the cause
A matter so small that, reflecting, we pause
To wonder how men of their metal could deem
Their precepts and prospects and friendly esteem
So easily blighted. The records, though dim,
Depict a good joke and a giddy girl's whim,
Which wrought the estrangement and brought by
        degrees
The challenge which nothing but blood might
        appease.

On yonder green isle of Missouri's dark soil
The field was selected, and swords without foil,

Keen-edged were the weapons, whose thrust
    neither feared;
The fighting arena was speedily cleared,
And there, in the shade of the towering trees,
Whose canopy waved in the murmuring breeze,
The distance was measured, each man to his place,
The referee called to attention and "face."

But then, as their weapons flashed forth into place,
A pitying protest was marked on each face
Of those who stood by, and, by common consent,
They cried as one voice the first blow to prevent;
And one, in behalf of the company, said—
A sunbeam enshrining his uncovered head:—
"By all you believe, friends, by those whom you
    love—
By Him who looks down on this scene from
    above—
By party and state and your own simple worth,
I pray you desist; cast your weapons to earth."

A flood of revulsion as strong as the tide
That rolled in the river so near to one side,
Swept over each heart as, with weapons at rest,
The duelists, clasping, their errors confessed.

A friendship was formed on that spot, which,
     though tried
In many political battles, defied
All thought of enstrangement. Each held in his day
Positions of power, and conquered his way
Through national conflict as bitter, and fraught
With venomous hate, as the battle they sought;
But, martyr and statesman, each willingly classed
The other in highest esteem to the last.

'Twas well for the nation that, by their own
     hands,
Their blood was not spilt on those dank river
     sands.
Their history is written, and each honored name
Preserved in the national archives of fame,
Rings down through the ages, a lesson sublime
Of manhood and progress that counts for all
     time.
The Father of Waters still washes to-day
The point where they met, as he rolls on his
     way;
And oft as the steamer goes laboring by,
The passenger seeks with inquisitive eye
Some landmark recalling, upon those green fields,
The bloodless encounter of Lincoln and Shields.

THE HOUSE WHERE I WAS BORN.

UPON the old familiar height,
    Time-stained and weather-worn,
It stands in hallowed majesty—
    The house where I was born.
I gaze upon it, deeply moved,
    And live, in fancy, o'er
The pleasant scenes and incidents
    Of youth, that's mine no more.

'Twas here I first beheld the light
    And found the world so fair,
Till young ambition, waked by love,
    Undid the clasp of care;
Here, too, I learned the earliest truth
    By blest surroundings taught,
And builded nobler works each day
    Than since my hands have wrought.

The casements in the sunset glow
  All burnished seem with gold,
And sparkle with reflected light
  Of memories bright and old;
E'en as the fading day was fair
  With all that makes complete,
Recalling of its brief career
  The story fond and sweet.

Ah, well, if, when my work is done,
  Others its worth shall see,
And grant that I have wrought as well
  As thou, old home, for me;
Whose influence still, my safest guide,
  Is with me every day;
An arm of strength and star of hope
  On life's uncertain way.

Those humble walls are rich compared
  With others gay and grand,
Holding a charm which none but one
  Who lived may understand.
No grace of Nature could enhance,
  Nor artist's touch adorn
The sacred halo that pervades
  The house where I was born.

PEARLS OF POESY.

OH, pearls of purest poesy,
  So beautiful and rare!
Could we but find their dwelling place,
  'Twere sweet to linger there,
'Mid scenes of radiant light and love,
  Where inspiration's fount
Springs up in rich abundance, from
  The heart of pleasure's mount.

But, even as the ocean pearls
  We cherish, dearly bought,
These jewels of the intellect,
  With life's best essence fraught,
Are only seldom captured from
  The deepest wells of thought.

'MID SCENES OF YOUTH.

BACK upon the dear old homestead, with the
    ones who love me well,
And each object wakes an echo of fond memories
    that swell
    Like a surging tide around me,
    Where my happy childhood found me,
Till my soul is wild within me with a joy I may
    not tell.

Every voice is rich with music, as of far-off
    minstrelsy,
And each tender thought, responsive, tells how
    good it is to be;
    'Tis an ecstasy as holy
    As the Christ-love, and as lowly
As the humble scenes that sanctify this hallowed
    spot for me.

Every landmark is familiar, and my heart, prone
     to enjoy,
Finds old friends with pulse ecstatic as it hailed
     its earliest toy;
   While each woodland whisper falling
   Seems an old companion calling
From the undulating pastures where I wandered
     as a boy.

All is rare and fair and fragrant, and awhile
     life's worries cease,
As the spirit unencumbered springs aloft in glad
     release;
   While a warmth beyond concealing
   Sounds the depths of fellow-feeling,
And I walk as one transported, in a realm of
     perfect peace.

A LESSON FOR LENT.

OH, rest from thy troubles, thou world-weary
    soul;
Embrace and find peace in the Lord;
Grieve not for thy failure to reach the longed goal,
    But turn to His comforting word.

The sorrows that sadden the journey of life
    Are mellowed by prayer's earnest pleas;
The longed-for relief from earth's jostle and strife
    The Savior's fond love will appease.

Whenever the Tempter entices away
    Thou'lt always find help at the throne;
And passions that rise in the world's bitter fray
    God quells and gives strength to disown.

CHRISTIAN WOMANHOOD.

TO A YOUNG LADY FRIEND ON HER UNITING WITH THE CHURCH.

YOU did not need to join the church
    To be and act a Christian's part,
For truth was always on your lips,
    And God dwelt ever in your heart.

And yet your brave admission comes
    Like a blest message from above—
An inspiration to the world
    Reflective of the Savior's love.

When woman's head is bowed in prayer,
    The listening angels pause to hear,
And each petition uttered there
    Shall echo through the boundless spheres.

Who knows how much of all the good
    Which man has compassed by degrees,
Was given in answer to the plea
    Of women on their bended knees,—

83

Whose intercessions never cease
    Their missions at the Throne of Grace,
Petitioning the Prince of Peace
    For favors to the human race.

Blest be the Christian woman's life:
    Heav'n ordained gift, on earth divine,
Since man, degenerate child of strife,
    First worshipped at its holy shrine.

BY THE RIVER.

AN ALLEGORY.

"OH, river that flowest so peacefully on,
    What is it I hear in thy mellow refrain
That comforteth me for the hopes that have
    flown,
    And bringeth the peace I have prayed for in
    vain?
Methinks as I list to thy murmuring song,
    Thou speakest in tones of condolence to me,
And bearest my turbulent spirits along,
    Confessing a bond of relation with thee."

"O, heart grown aweary with sorrow and care,
    Weep not for the dreams thou hast failed to
    attain,
What brooks it to yield to the voice of despair,
    Or mourn for the hopes we have cherished in
    vain?

We are but the children of Infinite will—
    Small atomic parts of the formative plan—
Performing the tasks we were sent to fulfill,
    And ending at last where at first we began.''

''Yet thou art so merry and singest of rest
    To me who am weary of life and its woes,
Reviving a hope in my sorrowing breast
    Of comfort and peace which this world never
        knows.
Hast thou never troubles to ruffle thy tide,
    That ever thou seemest so cheerful and gay
As on through the beautiful valley dost glide?
    Blest wanderer, tell me thy secret, I pray.''

''Yes, yes, dearest heart, I have troubles enow,
    As many, I trow, as thy pulse ever knew,
Yet ever fulfilling my duties I go,
    Refreshing the land while meandering through.
I nurture the fishes that bide on my breast,
    Support on my bosom the traffic of trade:
I am but a servant, yet service is blest,
    And duty accomplished goes never unpaid.

"Do therefore be patient and cease to complain,
    Fulfilling each duty with gentle accord,
Sure, nothing was ever created in vain,
    And time, in due season, will bring the reward.
Aye, down at the end of the journey we plod
    The haven is waiting for thee, friend, and me:
Thou goest to rest on the bosom of God,
    And I to my bed in the billowy sea."

THE SILVER WEDDING.

DEAR sweetheart, let us dream to-night the
    old dreams o'er again,
Recall once more the joyful throng that gathered
    round us then,
Just five-and-twenty years ago, when thou, my
    bonny bride,
First plighted me thy maiden troth here standing
    at thy side:
And I did promise all to thee that my fond heart
    could give,—
To cherish, honor, and protect, long as we both
    should live;
While fond ones pressed to wish us well, and
    sought to calm the fears
That overflowed through those dark eyes in half
    regretful tears.

So long ago, and yet, dear heart, it seems but
    yesterday,
Since erst you left your childhood's home and
    came with me away;

Much have we seen and felt since then of hap-
    piness and pain,
That left its threads of gray and gold in memory's
    silken skein:
Together we have loved and worked through
    swiftly passing years,
In fields of sunshine and success, and sorrow's
    vale of tears.
Thy tresses show the silver now, but yet thou
    art as fair
As when they wound the bridal wreath among
    thy raven hair.

And now, as on that day when first their blessings
    freely fell,
A merry circle gathers round, once more to wish
    us well;
But now they are our children dear, with faces
    fresh and fair,—
Fond hearts whose warm and tender love have
    well repaid our care.
Yes, all are gathered round the hearth, not one
    has gone away;
And listen, dear, for they would speak. What
    have they come to say!

89

"Kind parents, to whose constant care and all-
    enduring love
We owe a debt of gratitude which naught can
    e'er remove,
All that the coming years can give, to bless this
    quiet scene,
We fain would have them bring to cheer and
    grace your life serene;
And we will labor to fulfill the grateful thought
    we pray,
That you may live as happy till your golden
    wedding day."

THE TWO ANGLERS.

AWAY with dull duties, with business away!
   We're foot-loose for once, and are off for
      the day.
Out into the country with sunlight agleam,
'Mid infinite freedom of forest and stream.
Here scorn we the lore and the legends of books,
To study the science of tackle and hooks
With interest profound, that denotes this a sport
As rich as the rarest that mortal may court.
But even while luring with minnow and fly
The deep-water denizens, wary and shy,
E'en during the typical strike, while I feel
The weight of the captive that tugs at the reel,
A mem'ry of childhood, a vision of old,
Comes over me now, like a glimmer of gold
Athwart the horizon at set of the sun,
Recalling the dawn of a day that is done.
And, as with a glass, where the dim shadows meet,
I see a young hopeful, with unstockinged feet,
Steal over the stile to the pasture beyond,
To fish, though forbidden, down at the old pond.

Though years intervene 'twixt the boy and the man,
A kindred affinity bridges the span.
So quickly the latter is lost, and the lad
Revisits the scene which his elders forbade.
No day holds such promise, no skies are so fair,
No pleasure so perfect or nearly so rare;
No latest invention appeals to his soul
As those angle worms and the sassafras pole,
With cord-line and pin-hook he's wont to employ,
Whenever occasion permits it—the boy
Who down by the old pasture stile, and beyond,
Went fishin' for suckers in grandfather's pond.

MAMMA'S VALENTINES.

OF all the pretty valentines that circulate
    to-day,
Methinks by far the fairest are my little ones at
    play;
Nor aught of wit or sentiment these messengers
    convey
Can match my babies' pathos, or the cunning
    things they say.

There's more of joy in one brief hour of this dear
    trinity
Of faces bright as hope's own star, of life from
    guile so free;
And in these thumb-leaved nursery rhymes of
    sweet simplicity,
Than all the valentines that e'er the postman
    brought to me.

No thought by Cupid e'er transcribed on sta-
    tioner's designs,
Though laden with heart's treasures that o'er-
    flowed between the lines,
Was quite so pure and holy as the trusting love
    that shines
In every little sunny face of Mamma's valentines.

93

THE NOBLER CREED.

OH, Ingersoll, how hast thou taught
    That "death is but a dreamless sleep,"
And that life's pilgrimage is fraught
    With nothing sacred in our keep,—
That all our service may command
    Is that which may be compassed in
The span of earth's existence, and
    E'en "suicide is not a sin."

An' this be true, what recompense
    Were there for all the toil and pain,
Encountered here; what consequence
    Save that all strife, all hope were vain?
Then truly were all things but chance
    On this forlorn, terrestrial ball,
With life an aimless circumstance,
    And man the puppet of it all.

A nobler creed was his who penned
    The "Psalm of Life," whose lines extol
The truth that death is not the end
    Of life: "The tomb is not its goal."
How warms the heart to perfect trust
    In that divinely simple 'scroll;
Surmounting e'en the "dust to dust,"
    As never "spoken of the soul."

Indeed, who reads great Nature's book
    Can doubt not life's immortal dower;
The forest, field and running brook
    Teach resurrection every hour:
Who, then, would choose with Ingersoll
    His gloomy gospel of despair?
When "Hope" is written over all
    The earth, in lessons bright and fair.

OUT OF THE PAST.

IN listless mood I sat me down to rest
    Upon the lintel of an oaken door
Deserted years agone, and now possessed
    By clambering vines whose verdure covered o'er
The crumbling walls that framed the happy home
    Of sturdy pioneers, whose heirs to-day
Dwell in the shadow of yon towering dome,
    Where wealth is king, all else but common clay.

And musing here, methought I heard the chimes
    Of music soft, attuned to sturdy toil,
By those brave spirits of the early times
    Who drove the furrows through the virgin soil:
The glad refrain—ere gold and gilded sin
    Had caught the land in their dread undertow—
Of blithesome lives that drank the sunshine in;
    And cheery voices, hushed long, long ago.

CONVALESCENCE.

THERE came a robber into my home
    One dreary September day;
His name was Death, and he sought to steal
    The love of my life away.

Full armed was he in his sinister quest,
    To smite with remorseless hand,
And when I bade him begone, he scorned
    The plea of my rash demand.

The world was drear in mine eyes that day,
    Though brightly the sun did shine,
Hope's lamp burned low, and the birds' glad song
    Seemed nothing at all divine.

* * *

But faith is stronger than fate, I ween,
    And love than a moment's fears;
Through Him, who orders the tide of life
    And shapeth the course of years.

The hand that threatened was turned aside,
 And into the house there came
A boundless joy when my darling woke,
 And smiled as I spoke her name.

Her dear face glows by the hearth once more
 And, marry, this heart of mine
Hears, 'mid the sough of the autumn gale,
 The lilt of a song divine.

BLIGHTED.

BUT yester' eve I proudly strolled
　　Among the greening orchard trees,
Bedecked with bursting buds that told
　　Of mellowy fruits in all degrees.
Methought I saw the harvest time
　　Already dawning, and the air
Forescented by the summer's thyme,
　　With plenty smiling everywhere.
So happy in the promised yield,
　　I held it e'en as certain gain,
And all that fancy's flight revealed
　　I counted in mine own domain.

Alack! to-day I walked again
　　Those orchard rows, how sadly changed!
Where all was growth and promise then
　　Is naught of either.　All estranged
The landscape seems, and crumpled leaves,
　　Their symmetry and beauty gone,
Like prematurely gathered sheaves,
　　Droop from the boughs they grew upon.

On every hand is quick decay—
    Sad sequence of the Frost King's blight,—
By whom the buds of yesterday
    Were blasted in a single night.

So have I seen the fairest hope
    That blossomed in the heart of youth,
Crushed out in its divinest scope
    And withered by the fires of ruth.
What lesson, what example here?
    What recompense for so much pain?
The stricken flower, the smarting tear,
    How can we count its passing gain?
We may not tell; we are but blind;
    We trust because we cannot know,
That in this loss we still may find
    The wiser plan which willed it so.

THE COMING OF THE BRIDE.

THE peace that comes of perfect love
    And warms the constant heart,
Be o'er this home and bless this hour
    With all its vows impart,
While we are gathered, as of old,
    Responsive Nature stayed,
When angels wrote the plighted troth
    Of first fond man and maid.

Obedient to the master touch,
    The ivory keys proclaim
A happier triumph than was e'er
    Achieved on field of fame,
For ne'er was holier circumstance
    By music ratified,
Than when the wedding march proclaims
    The coming of the bride.

The hopes and fears of other years—
  The day-dreams that have sped,
Are vanished like the summer dews
  That bowed the lily's head;
The vague regrets and might-have-beens
  That vex the youthful breast,
Are merged in blessed certainty
  That that which is, is best,

Florescent sprays of mignonette,
  The pansy's graceful pose,
The drooping branch of bleeding heart
  That blushes with the rose,
Are symbolized in yon pure gift
  Of Flora's fairest dower,
That sanctifies this circle with
  Its crown of orange flower.

And as, anon, the clergyman
  With voice distinct and slow,
Conducts the solemn services
  That join for weal or woe,
The loftiest pledge that language e'er
  Has turned to human skill,
Twice spoken, seals the compact with
  The glad response, "I will."

Amen! We greet the bride and groom,
　　And wish them, with the flow
Of life's fleet tide, a peaceful cruise,
　　Inspired as we go
To draw the portieres of our hearts
　　About this love-lit scene,
And pray, "God bless them through the course
　　Of years that intervene."

THE SCHOOL-HOUSE ON THE HILL.

DOWN the lane and up the valley, through
    the pasture by the mill,
Lies the pathway, and I follow, as it were, a
    child at will,
Till it ends beneath the belfry of the school-
    house on the hill.

Like a hymn of consecration, and with meaning
    as complete
As the score of rude initials carved upon the
    rearmost seat,
Are the merry peals of laughter and the rush of
    nimble feet

On the playground, as I linger, fain to be a boy
    again,
And forgetful of the changes that have marked
    my way since then—
Innocent of all the worries of this world of busy
    men.

As by some magician's challenge, all the past is
      swept away,
And the boys and girls of forty are the children
      of to-day,
In this hour of intermission, given up to joyous
      play.

Some contending in the forum to redeem the
      Golden Rule,
Some are weaving webs of fancy from tradition's
      mystic spool;
Others, passed to broader vision in a better,
      higher school,

Since they heard that bell at recess sound its
      summons, as sublime
And as potent in its echoes down the endless
      course of Time,
As the Sabbath morning message of the grandest
      steeple chime.

Seems as if the voice of conscience, speaking
      through that oaken door,
Would reproach me as unworthy of the lessons
      learned of yore—
That those precepts should have fruited in a fund
      of riper lore.

Yet, a deeper sense assures me that whate'er I
    may have wrought
Worthy of commemoration in the argosies of
    thought,
Grew e'en from this humble temple where my
    A. B. C.'s were taught.

Every memory is sacred, and the eye of fancy sees
Joy or penitence responsive to the teacher's stern
    decrees;
And what pastimes! From the ball-field to the
    jolly spelling bees.

Through the mist of life's emotions it conveys a
    subtle thrill;
So, God grant that in the gloaming I may see it
    standing, still,
And inhale the inspiration of the school-house on
    the hill.

GLAD EASTER TIME.

HAIL the resurrection anthems
    Sounding merrily and free,
As of old their music echoed
    O'er the tide of Gallilee;
Heralding the final triumph
    Over sorrow and the tomb,
Sung by every voice of nature,
    Symbolized in every bloom
That adorns the smiling landscape
    On this merry Easter morn,
Bright with hope and fair with promise
    Of a higher life, new-born.

Bringing peace to all the nation
    Through the grace of love divine,
Warming every Christian spirit,
    Like the thrill of sacred wine:

With the pulse of fellow feeling
    In the pleasure we impart,
By the gifts which bless the giver,
    Sending joy to every heart;
Happy in the glad fulfillment,
    Told in every steeple chime,
Of the promises of Christmas
    In the fact of Easter time.

A CAMP-SIDE REVERIE.

FORGETTING all the world's affairs,
  Its endless, vexing grind of cares,
Perplexities and cunning snares:
    Recumbent by the fire
Of smouldering logs, on summer night,
Just thinking, by the flickering light,
Good, lazy thoughts; to what delight
    More pure could man aspire?

With nothing to disturb the mind,
Lulled and caressed by whisp'ring wind,
Here may the spirit, self-resigned,
    Repose in perfect peace;
Where life's elixir comes unsought,
Borne in the breezes, fragrance fraught,
By every touch of nature taught,
    'Mid songs that never cease.

Songs of the insects, soft and sweet,
Frogs in the waters at thy feet,
And night-birds in their dark retreat,
    All help to weave the spell,
Whose charm surcharges all my heart
With subtle joy, the rarest art
Of worded language to impart
    Has not the power to tell.

No monarch in his princely bower
E'er reveled in a richer hour,
Nor found the subjects of his power
    More tractile to his wish,
Than I in this Arcadian dream,
While pondering many a subtle scheme
For luring from his native stream
    My finny friend, the fish.

THE FISH WE FAILED TO LAND.

THROUGH the early twilight shadows, singing
in falsetto shrill,
Comes an urchin o'er the meadows from the
creek across the hill;
Nimble footed, though so tired from his romps
along the stream,
Like a hero, self-inspired, while his dark eyes
fairly gleam
With exultant animation as he holds aloft his
"string,"
And begins his proud narration, with the crafts-
man's coloring.
And he tells us, bidding slyly for another holiday,
Of the catch of Jimmy Riley and what whoppers
got away!
Then—observe the tone of sorrow, as he lays the
tempting lure—
If he might but go to-morrow he could do much
better, sure.

How his daft adroitness moves you with a
    kindred feeling deep;
And a subtle sense reproves you, as you say,
    "The fish will keep."
For the voice of memory reasons from those little
    sunburned feet,
Backward through a score of seasons thronged
    with happenings sad and sweet,
Ruminating fancy lingers over many a fickle dream
That has slipped between your fingers since you
    fished in yonder stream;
And you read the grave condition, which this lad
    is yet untaught,—
In the shade of each ambition and the recompense
    it brought;—
That the life of man forever echoes to some vain
    regret,
And its bravest, best endeavor was the fish he
    failed to get.

THE HUNTSMAN.

UP in the morn with the first peep of daylight,
    Out in the meadows ahead of the sun;
Off for a respite from dull office duties,
    Over the hills with dog, tackle and gun.

Buoyant and free as the breezes of autumn,
    Murmuring soft over woodland and wold;
Tingles each fiber with anticipation,
    Watching each moment a mark to behold.

Up and away, jovial and gay,
    Far from the grind of care, calm in his glee;
Over the field, pleasure must yield,
    Joy to the hunter, contented and free.

List! over yonder the partridge is calling,
    Hear how he thrashes the air with his wings;
Steady! well done! see the bird lightly falling,
    Caught by my trusty retriever; he springs

Back and away where the covey has settled,
    What tho' we miss them, the sport is the same;
Failure but sharpens the sportman's ambition;
    Lives there a man of infallible aim?

Thus goes the day; tell me, I pray,
    Is there a pastime as healthful and free?
Truce to all sport others may court,
    Gun, field and dog are the fairest for me.

Or if the scene be the river or marshland,—
    Whether for feathered or four-footed game,—
So but success crown the earnest endeavor,
    Matters but little, the pleasure's the same.

Sing who may list of the ball-field's attractions,
    Games that have flourished awhile and declined;
None may compare with the pleasures that, hidden,
    Fostered by Nature, here 'wait who shall find.

List to the horn, fresh on the morn,
    Echoing clear over woodland and lea,
Seek if you will elsewhere, but still
    Forest and field are the fairest for me.

NOT IN THE PAST.

NOT in the past, 'midst fallen thrones,
    Haunted by ghosts of vanished power,
Can we find answers for the needs
    And questions of the present hour.

Not he is great who idly mourns
    The downfall of an ancient State,
But he who strives and thinks to save
    His country from as dark a fate.

Muse not on haughty Cæsar's rule,
    Whose bones long since returned to clay;
But in the present busy world
    Be thou the Cæsar of to-day.

O, dreamer in the aisles of Time,
    Arouse thee from thy reverie,
Awake! Come to the front and fight
    For thy own home and liberty:
Turn from the ruins of the past
    To that which is, and is to be!

MONOTONE.

OH, monotone,—of warring words
    That echo to life's vain appeal,
Or weave their phantom frames about
    The image of each lost ideal,—
Of winds that whistle evermore,
    And seem to mock, malignantly,
All things that bide upon the earth
    And, fettered, struggle to be free.

Oh, voice of Nature, vast and lone,
    Though by each passing sound instilled,
Gathered through all the ages flown,
    And with quintescent sadness filled;
Like some lost spirit making moan
    For every promise, unfulfilled.

THE IMAGE BREAKER.

STAND back! thou rash iconoclast!
  Lift not thy prodding spade to blast
Yon sacred temple of the dead!
What wouldst thou with the weapons dread
That guard this long-lost people's dust?
To pander an ignoble lust,
And steal the secrets of the past!
No grave can hold its treasure fast;—
No fame so high, no shrine so pure—
No hallowed image is secure
Against the sacrilegious blade
That marks the relic-hunter's trade!

In every nook of every land
Are works of his defacing hand;
And why? What has he for his toil?
A pile of useless, crumbling spoil,
Which cannot serve one worthy end,
Much less his lawless work defend.

O, cease, traducer of the grave,
Leave to the past her rusted glave;
Leave them in peace—these mummied things—
And study truth from living springs;
Confine thyself to modern bounds,
And let tradition guard these mounds.

TO A TREE FROG.

SAUCY little elfin prophet,
　　Challenging the thirsty wold
From its fitful mid-day slumber
　　With thy croaking, harsh and bold—
How dost know a storm is brewing,
　　When no cloud is in the sky?
And each drooping thing about thee
　　Seems to give thee back the lie?

Hast some subtle intuition
　　In thy secret cell of bark?
Or a mystic cipher message
　　From the Rain God's distant ark?
Or art merely telling falsely
　　To awaken doubt and strife?
If so, and I had thee captive,
　　It should quickly cost thy life,

Nay, but I believe thee, truly;
　　Thou wast reared in Nature's heart,
Where no falsehood e'er is nourished,
　　And shouldst know thy single art
Over more pretentious prophets:
　　Else thy lot were wholly vain.
All athirst the world is waiting,
　　Speed the promise—let it rain.

THE LESSON OF COLUMBUS.*

"COLUMBUS!" how the chorus swells in
  honor to the name,
As on this festal day we meet to celebrate his
  fame,
And fling the flags of freedom on the sombre
  autumn breeze,
E'en as of old they waved for him upon the
  friendly seas,
As from the court of Spain his ships went out
  with sails unfurled,
To battle with the elements and find another world.

Four hundred years ago, and yet it does not
  seem so long:
The memory is so well preserved in history and
  song;
Each child has heard the story of that earnest,
  fearless man,
Who braved a thousand unknown deaths to verify
  his plan,
That, far beyond the Western skies, where none
  had gone before,
The sun that seemed to dip the wave, shone on
  some fairer shore.

---

*NOTE XI.—Appendix.

A mighty thought it was, than which no nobler
    e'er was known;
And greater still the master mind that faced the
    world alone,
With fortitude to bear the taunts of unbelief,
    and then
Persuade a doubting monarch to provide the
    means and men
To prove his theory correct, or forfeit with his own,
Those other lives, and bring reproof upon the
    Spanish throne.

Thus from the life which gave the world this
    Western hemisphere
We learn our noblest lesson still,—to dare and
    persevere.
All that we have achieved since then is from that
    precept drawn,
Still nerving us to better deeds and pointing on
    and on:
E'en as of old Columbus' ships, with silken sails
    unfurled,
Were guided o'er the trackless deep to find
    another world.

BALLAD OF THE BRAVE.

HARK! hark to the beating
  Of music repeating
The charge for the meeting
  Of armies of old.
But softly, more slowly,
More hallowed and holy,
Each patriot bows lowly
  Whenever 'tis told;—

The story recalling
Of battles befalling
With carnage appalling
  From sabre and shell;
Where heroes unbending
For honors contending,
Their colors defending,
  Fought, conquered and fell.

This day does the Nation
In proud celebration
Of commemoration,
    Bring flowers and tears,
Their graves fondly strewing,
And praises renewing,
The fame of whose doing
    Fades not with the years.

Old comrades repeating,
Ere once more retreating,
The bivouac's greeting
    Above the green mold;
And they, in their glory
Of battle-fields gory,
Sleep on through the story
    That never grows old.

ONCE MORE WITH REJOICING.

ONCE more with rejoicing, fair day, in thy
    glory,
  We welcome the memories thy echoes recall;
From pulpit and stage we repeat the glad story,
    How freedom first echoed through liberty's hall.
        In glad celebration
        The sons of the nation
Assemble again 'neath the red, white and blue—
        With memories glowing,
        And hearts overflowing.
With all that is loyal and tender and true.

'Tis meet that we come thus in fancy reviewing
    The scenes where was planted fair liberty's tree,
Each young generation the pledges renewing
    That made our country "the land of the free;"
        With rocket and rattle
        Repeating the battle
Wherein the oppressor was conquered and fell;
        Each stroke from the steeple
        And shout of the people
Recalling the chimes of the Liberty bell.

Dear land for whose welfare our fathers have striven,
  To free thee forever from tyranny's rod
Thy past we bequeath to the keeping of heaven—
  Thy future we trust to the mercy of God.
      With hearts proudly beating,
      Hozannas repeating,
We leave thee again to the guidance Divine;
      May wars never scatter
      Thy homesteads, or shatter
The banner that waves over Liberty's shrine.

LIFE'S RURAL WAY.

FAR from the city's noisome scenes away
    Happy are those who thread earth's rural way.
Not in the crowd that throngs the busy street,
Among the fleeting faces that we meet;
Not in the whirl of the commercial mart,
The school of pleasure or the hall of art,
Nor anywhere in this chaotic round
Is life's complete fulfillment ever found,

Go ye who this most fragrant flower would find,
Of sweet contentment to the soul and mind,
Go seek where nature's bounty freely yields
The restful opulence of sunny fields;
Aye, go and be as yonder sturdy swain
Who knows or cares not that his dress is plain,
Whose best ambition from his daily toil
To glean the product of the native soil.

Nothing to him is fashion's frail regard,
The thirst for office or its false reward: .
He worships fortune with his own right hand;
Is self-dependent,—bows to no command,—
And spurns the dullard who presumes to scorn
The honest value of an ear of corn.

With him to dwell among the orchard trees,
Inhale the fragrance of the fruitful breeze,
Or in the woods, of other days to dream,
Soothed by the ripple of some pasture stream;
Here dwells the peace of pleasure most profound,
Spiced by the salt of duty's daily round.
Blessed beyond the common ken are they
Who thus elect to tread life's rural way.

LIKE AS A STAR.

I STOOD upon the vernal height
    Of youth, and gazing out afar,
Beheld the iridescent light
    Of Fortune, like a shooting star;
Harnessed to hopes that in their reach
    Outspanned the noblest mind's desire;
And which, translated into speech,
    Would glow with inspiration's fire.

Then, looking down, I saw below
    A shadow flitting in the dark,
And threading cables to and fro
    To drag to earth that shining mark.
To rise or fall—to wane or shine,
    Such is the struggle, passing o'er;
Transcendent as a light divine,
    Or falling, to be seen no more.

E'en such is life—an orb of light
    Drifting athwart the vault of Time;
A day-star jeweled in the night
    Of earth's dark ways—a spark sublime
That, tending upwards in its course,
    And growing still to more and more,
Would thrill the droning world, and force
    Its light beyond the finite shore.

But in the shadow-lands of sin
    There lurk the demons of despair,
Weaving their webs of doubt, wherein
    Bright spirits find their fatal snare.
'Twixt hope to rise, and fear to fall—
    So passes every mortal span;
While One, presiding over all,
    Works out the great Creative Plan.

WHAT MIGHT NOT BE.

NAY, do not think me cold of heart
    Because I never spoke of love;
Nor charge me with so base a part
    As these old letters seem to prove.
Friends let us be, as erst we were;
    And though we may not quite forget,
Let naught that others may aver
    Bring back to us one vain regret.

Had I but dared, I might have told—
    But no, this cannot help us now:
    Duty forbade that sacred vow.
Perchance the future yet may hold
    For us some sweet reward in store,
    When love illumes a brighter shore.

HEROES UNREVEALED.

WHO said our heroes all were gone?
  Not so! By heaven, 'tis untrue!
Ye measure but what men have done,
  ·And not what others yet may do.

True, those were brave who fought our wars
  And, honor-crowned, have gone to rest,
But then it needs not battle scars
  The spirit's valor to attest.

The land has many sons as brave,
  Who never saw the bloody field,
As those who faced a nameless grave
  Their country's flag from shame to shield.

Though yet, perchance, it sleeps unkenned—
  Uncalled, and therefore unconfessed,
Let but Columbia call: "Defend!"
  The fire will blaze in every breast.

"To arms!" let once the trumpet peal,
  And mark the answering host immense:
With courage strong and hearts as leal
  As ever fought in her defense.

IN THE OLD PRISON CEMETERY.

HARK, to the beat of myriad feet that over hill
 and dell
Come to dispose the graves of those who for
 their country fell!
Sad recompense for their defence of this fair land
 of ours;
We go each year with grateful tears, and strew
 their graves with flowers.
With fife and drum again we come, and flags
 unfurled to view,
As erst they came, and laud their fame—the boys
 who wore the blue.

But where are they who wore the gray and
 perished far from home,
Whose life, enthralled in prison walls, went out
 unwept, unknown?
Fond hearts that yearned for their return were
 anxious all in vain,
Straining the view till their life, too, went out in
 silent pain.

Unmarked to-day they sleep, and, aye, the voice
    of love is mute;
None visit here, with flowers and tears, to fire
    the grave's salute;
Yet who may tell but, just as well, they rest
    beneath the moss,
As those whose bed is heralded by towering
    shaft and cross?
The stone that marks the soldier's rest, here
    'neath the greening sod,
Points from these quiet meadows, through the
    shadows, up to God.

A WORD.*

A WORD, a breath, that scarcely moves,
  Which to no soul one tremor brings—
A word, that shakes earth's deepest grooves
  And bears the whirlwind on its wings.

A word, a sound, in earnest spoken,
  That thrills the heart with quickening touch,
Has oft united, oft has broken—
  A word, so little yet so much.

'A word of doom; ah! who knows whether
  He hath not lengthened that dark scroll?
A word of love, like unctioned feather,
  It heals some weary, wounded soul.

A word of light, illumes the mountain,
  Or shrouds the vale of life's reverse.
A word! 'tis joy's or sorrow's fountain:
  A benediction, or a curse.

THE SUBMERGED CITY.*

FROM the ocean's depths 'mid sea-weeds
    springing,
  Curfew bells are ringing soft and low,
To the sailors' eyes strange tidings bringing
  Of the grand old town that lies below.

Deep within the heaving depths of the ocean
  Are its turrets standing far below,
And above them is the billow's motion
  Lighted with a strange and fitful glow.

And the sailor who, at sunset peering,
  Saw the magic light from off the shore,
In that same direction still is steering,
  Though the billows round him madly roar.

* * *

From my heart's deep fountains, sadly springing,
  Memory's bells are ringing soft and low;
To my sea-sick soul strange tidings bringing
  Of the dear old friends of long ago.
Ah! a beauteous city there lies sleeping—
  Like a glimpse of paradise it seems—
Oft when I beheld its turrets, weeping,
  In the blessed mirror of my dreams.

A THRENODY OF TEARS.

REPRESS not the bright tear that dims thine eye,
  Since, dear, I know that it was meant for me:
May I but kiss the love-lit token dry
  That trembles on thy lids so witchingly!
Through tears like these angelic spirits shine,
And I would know thee never less divine.

Yet every tear, alas, betokens pain,
  And is the sign of tender soul's unrest;
And I do pray thee, dearest, to refrain
  From judgment, if my tongue hath seemed to jest.
Claim thou my heart's blood, who hast wept for me,
And hold me still for aye in debt to thee.

Sometimes, when others dared to call me base,
  And sinister hatred barred my humble way;
I found sweet inspiration in thy face,
  As angels pure, who at God's footstool pray.
And were I bad at heart as they have said,
No seraph for me had bowed her weeping head.

Peace, darling, I will dry them, every one—
    The tears thou'st wept on this devoted breast,—
Thus they have gone: their holy work is done,
    And through the pain there comes love's per-
      fect rest.
Nay, weep no more—and at God's altar fair,
I'll weave the myrtle in thy silken hair.

A SONG OF LABOR DAY.

TO-DAY the toilers of the land, with sturdy
 voice and tread,
Proclaim how good a thing it is to strive for
 honest bread.
A mighty bannered host they march, like veterans
 to the wars,
And proudly every man salutes the nation's stripes
 and stars:
Nor grander army e'er went forth to fight in
 Freedom's name,
Than they who on this festal day their loyalty
 proclaim
To home and country, church and State,—to
 every grace that gives
Each man the ample blessings of the sphere in
 which he lives.

Though military armament and code be missing
 here,
Much more there is of hope and faith, much less
 of doubt and fear;

Where every man a soldier is, to follow and
     command,
Himself a host; his battlefield, the labors of his
     hand.

Honor the hero and the time, and let forensic art
Rehearse the lessons and the truths which are its
     highest part.
Proud is the nation in her strength, but proudest
     most of those
Who make her fields and factories, and to whose
     might she owes
The garnered wealth that makes her great—by
     whose support she stands
Above all others of the earth, the queen of happy
     lands.
Be this the motto of the hour: " 'Tis noblest to
     be true,
With hand and heart to every task that duty
     brings us to."

DEFERRED.

LOOK you at yon two radiant orbs
    Approaching in the Western sky,
So closely that their light absorbs
    The space between, to mortal eye.
We gaze across the distance and
    In fancy see the stars embrace;
Pleased, though we may not understand
    This love scene in the realms of space.
But mark how brief the tryst has been;
    Where lately they appeared as one,
Now shines a streak of gold between,
    Reflected from the setting sun,
Yes, Nature's laws. must be obeyed,
    E'en here as in the lives of men,
And years shall lengthen to decades,
    Ere yon two planets meet again.

So have I known—pray who has not?—
    Two souls that for each other seemed
Designed: whose every act and thought
    Each in the other's self redeemed.

And here, methought, is one ideal
    Of poets dreamed, in fact fulfilled;
While, gazing on their bliss so real,
    My soul with kindred rapture thrilled.
Alas, when next I looked, a spell
    Of sadness on each face was set,
Betraying, as they said, "Farewell,"
    The shadow of a life's regret.
Yet purpose rules the orb of earth,
    And 'spite of all its purchased pain,
The hopes that fade in sorrow's dearth,
    Though long deferred, are not in vain.

SING WE OF LOVE.

"LONG, long ago, love,"
    Thus runs the song;
Sweetly the music
    Ripples along.
Hark! how the rhythm,
    Tender and slow,
Echoes our young love,
    Long, long ago.

What does it teach us,
    Love, can you hear?
Borne in the measure
    Year after year;
Seasons of gladness—
    Moments of woe—
Whereof we dreamed not
    Long, long ago.

Have we regrets, love?
    E'en did we stray
Near to the edge of
    Life's pleasant way?

Be this forgotten;
    How could we know
Where there was danger
    Long, long ago?

Such is love's guerdon—
    Counting as gain
Every achievement
    Compassed through pain.
Therefore we sing, since
    God willed it so,
Happier now than
    E'en, long ago.

THE SILENT SENTINEL.

AS the picket lone who, stationed,
  When the army rests at large,
Guards the sleeping camp from danger
  By the foemen's stealthy charge,
Stands the conscience in the vanguard
  Of the mind's defensive host,
Challenging each doubtful motive
  That would pass the outer post.

Safe the heart while conscience, faithful,
  Watches on the outer wall,
And each better pulse responsive,
  Rallies at the warning call,
But the soul is deep in danger
  If this guardian flinch or fall.

THE MUSIC OF THE WHEEL.

OFT while waiting slumber's coming
    I have listened to the drumming,
As of some great bee-hive humming,
    Of the steamer's ponderous wheel;
And the troubled waters gushing,
In their pent-up quarters flushing,
As if anxious, in their rushing,
    To escape the rudder's heel.

How the paddles' rhythmic measure
Hurls the foam from their embrasure,
Seemingly in savage pleasure,
    With each turning of the wheel;
While the river, gliding under
With a swell like distant thunder,
Brings suggestive thoughts to ponder
    Till the senses fairly reel!

Thus the mighty palpitation
And the dull reverberation
Time the steady oscillation
    Of the massive shafts of steel,
Until Fancy goes off dancing,
Into Dreamland's shadows prancing,
Like the spray-beat waves aglancing
    From the vessel's flying keel.

HYPOCRISY.

NOT from the round of mortal cares
    The worry of the world's affairs,
Its open pits and hidden snares;
From obstacles that block life's way
As down the path from day to day
Toward the final goal we stray,
    Would I most fain be free:

But from the cant of party schools,
The babble of pedantic fools,
The senseless sway of Fashion's rules;
From friends who do not sympathize,
Who poison grief with hollow sighs
And flatter truth with conscious lies,—
    From these deliver me.

THE BATTLE OF BRAINS.

NAPOLEON stood grieving on Helena's isle;
    He thought of his forfeited crown,
And of the mistake in the battle which turned
    The tide of his life and renown.
"Had Grouchy not failed me," he bitterly said,
    "We could not have lost, that is plain;
The French would have won and the vultures of war
    Had feasted on Wellington's brain."

Life is but a bivouac, the world is its field,
    And men are all soldiers of fame,
Who struggle for points of position and place,
    Where honors are fraught with acclaim.
Engagements are many, and skirmishes oft
    Take place on disputed domain,
But all the great victories counting for time
    Are wrought through the battle of brain.

This greatest of conflicts the world ever knew
    Is waging forever and aye;
Wherever men meet, e'en in labors of love,
    They join in the ceaseless affray.
Each grapples his neighbor and struggles with might
    Some stealthy advantage to gain,
And one must go down—inexorable tide
    Of fate in this conquest of brain.

Each man is a private, enlisted for life,
    Or drafted for service in youth,
And none may avoid it, e'en bodily ills
    Commend nor exemption or ruth.
Though thousands disabled are sent to the rear,
    Their trouble ends not in the pain:
Aye! still unavoidable unto the last,
    It rages—the battle of brain.

Here are no deserters, nor bushwhacking clans,
    For none may avoid or invade
The code of fair conquest, and yet, in the end
    All soldiers are pensioned and paid.
Each one is rewarded as he may achieve,
    And none ever conquered in vain,
And leisure and pleasure are guerdon for all
    Who win the great battle of brain.

IN AFTER YEARS.

LET us walk again, dear Allie,
 Down the peaceful twilight valley;
O'er the lealand to the pebble-garnished shore,
 Where the evening lights are gleaming,
 And thy poet's fancy, dreaming,
Like the love of other years, has gone before.

 Thinking of the sweet old story,
 When, by yonder promontory,
Thou didst own the dear regard that made thee mine,
 Thrills my soul with subtle sadness,
 Born of all those years of gladness,
Like the sparkling after-taste of seasoned wine.

 While the harbor wind's low droning
 All the tenderness is owning
That companionship hath brought to thee and me;
 And the voice of memory calling,
 On the ear so softly falling,
As the ceaseless, mellow sounding of the sea.

148

Time hath fled, dear, since the season
    When, by love's exquisite reason,
First we walked the beach together, hand in hand;
    Yet our course hath had no turning
    Since I stooped and, thrilled with yearning,
Marked our monogram upon the shifting sand.

    Youth is fickle, time is fleeting,
    Every pleasure is retreating,
And the heart may sleep to-night that warms to-day;
    But for us the pristine glory
    Ne'er shall fade from life's fond story,
Who abide, each in the other, while we may.

WHEN THE HOUSEWIFE IS AWAY.

ALL the house is strangely dreary,
    That was always erst so cheery,
And a something sad and eerie
    Dwells within, that seems to say:
"There is none here to reprove us,
Much less challenge and remove us
From the shadowy nooks that love us,
    Since the housewife is away."

Seems the bric-a-brac all tarnished,
And the furniture unvarnished,
Every article dust-garnished,
    Never so until to-day;
There is chaos from the table
To the rusted kitchen ladle,
And, alack! the empty cradle
    Tells that mamma is away.

Not the blissful daily meeting,
Nor one word of kindly greeting,
No familiar sound repeating
    Save the saucy mice at play;
And the husband lingers only
To select a hearth more homely,
For the house is all too lonely
    When the little wife's away.

A WINTER'S STORM.

DARK is the sky, of inky hue,
    Lost every faintest gleam of light;
No friendly star appears in view
    To cheer us with its presence bright,
For once the prophecies were true,—
    The storm-king is abroad to-night.
The wind, like some lost, living thing,
    Moans 'round the house with doleful screech;
Sets every timber shuddering,
    Chastising all within its reach;
Threshes the river with its wing,
    And hurls the breakers on the beach.

Trembles the earth beneath the strain
    And seems to plead for clemency,
Spurned by the storm in cold disdain,
    Which laughs aloud in savage glee;
While from the lowering clouds, the rain
    Is swept in torrents o'er the lea.
God help the vessel, gone amiss,
    That rides the deep with sails unfurled
Amid the roaring tempest's hiss:
    And 'fend each soul by fate imperiled
To wander, on a night like this,
    Homeless and friendless through the world!

IF WE WERE YOUNG AGAIN.

"THINK you," my dear wife said to me,
   One evening as we sat at tea,
"Would we as fond and foolish be
   If we were young again?"
"Methinks it surely could not be,
   And we would live as merrily,
   With less of youth's frivolity,
   If we were young again.

"How many an endless debt we owe
   For inconsiderate 'yes' or 'no,'
   That surely we would now forego
   If we were young again;
   And looking backward o'er life's plain,
   What gloomy days, what bitter pain
   Are there, that might be lasting gain
   If we were young again.

" 'Twere sweet to walk those thymy ways
    With lowlier hearts, more prone to praise,
    And leave no rue for later days—
        If we were young again."
"Nay, love," I answered, "age is prone
    To censure from its sombre throne
    As faults, acts we would proudly own
        If we were young again.

"Forgetting how it grew to be,
    It views, through glasses, scornfully,
    Motes of misconduct none might see
        If we were young again;
    Those foibles of the early years,
    Chastened by riper joys and tears,
    Temper the whole, which God reveres—
        Though we were young again.

"Those acts we now would fain recall
    Would hold us in their pleasant thrall,
    Nor would we deem them strange, withal,
        If we were young again.
    Nay, we would scorn youth's Paradise,
    Discover with the self-same eyes,
    But just as foolish—and as wise,—
        If we were young again."

THE ROSE.

I PLUCKED a rose with careless hand,
  Gazed on its perfect charms unmoved,
And, marking scarce that it was fair,
  I gave it to the girl I loved.
She took it with a gracious smile
  That might dispel the deepest gloom,
And, holding up the trembling thing,
  Bade me inhale its sweet perfume.

As I obeyed her dear behest
  I caught a scent so sweet and rare
It seemed sublime, and which before
  I had not dreamed lay hidden there.
She pinned it fast, when I beheld
A thousand beauties it possessed,
  Yet which I ne'er had marked until
I saw it blushing on her breast.

Ah! woman, such thy mission here,
    Sent as a blessing to the earth
To find for us each fragrant flower
    That blooms amid life's dross and dearth,
Our natures are too coarsely strung,
    Our days too full of busy hours
To note, unprompted, and enjoy,
    The fragrance of the wayside flowers.

Man has not any joys on earth—
    No hour of pure and perfect glee,—
O woman, pearl of priceless worth,
    That does not, somehow, come from thee.
Thyself the fairest flower of all
    That man may worship in his day,
Thy mission is to help and bless
    And cheer him on his weary way.

SEPTEMBER SYMPHONIES.

NOW comes the mellow time of year,
    When o'er the smiling land
The genius of the harvest rides
    And casts, with bounteous hand,
The golden fruits of labor to
    The gleaners of the field,
Whose honest hearts o'erflow with thanks
    For each abundant yield.

Now calls again the whippoorwill,
    And in the ripened grass
The crickets and the katydids
    Repeat their nightly mass.
The quail is piping in the woods,
    And by the river's edge
The bull-frog croaks his plaintive lay
    Among the broken sedge.

The ripening nuts begin to fall,
    The leaves to lose their sheen,
Each towering monarch of the woods
    Puts on a duller green.
Anon the stiffening breezes bring
    Their warning o'er the wold,
Jack Frost is riding down the wind
    With Winter's chariot cold.

THE FAIREST SCENE.

ONE night I sat and mused alone,
    Enraptured, in a trance serene;
I thought of all the sorrows flown,
    And all the pleasures I had seen.
Fair visions passed before my view,—
    The ghosts of revels I had kept—
Till, wearied of the long review,
    My eyes grew heavy and I slept.

And then methought an angel came
    And stood beside me in the gloom;
About her forehead played a flame
    That sent a halo through the room.
She cast a kindly glance at me,
    Then touched my hand and whispered low:
"Come, go with me and you shall see
    The fairest scene that earth can show."

I followed her across the green,
    And onward through a lonely wood,
To where, amid the peaceful scene,
    A shade-embowered cottage stood,
Nestled among the swaying trees.
    She drew the blinds and sweetly smiled:
Within, a mother on her knees
    Was praying for her sleeping child.

PILGRIM'S PRAYER.

GOD lend us light
And teach us right,
And lead us safely through the night
Of life's dark way,
Lest we should stray
From home and hope of Heaven away.

Teach us to see
Our liberty
As blessings coming all from Thee,
And grant us skill
With strength and will,
To climb to nobler conquests still.

Thy grief forbear
If tempting snare
Has e'er misled us anywhere;
Nor grant Thy wrath
This aftermath
If we have tarried by the path.

Inspire us yet
Lest we forget
The landmarks where our journey's set;
And on and on,
By duty drawn,
Conduct us towards a fairer dawn.

So hold us fast,
Until at last
The final milestone has been passed:
Then, safe and blest,—
Our faults confessed,—
Within Thy Kingdom give us—rest.

IN LATE OCTOBER.

HOW grand, beyond comparison, these late
    October days,
Wrapped in the mellow drapery of the Indian
    Summer's haze?
'Tis pleasure's purest essence now upon some
    crowning hill
To stand and drink the beauties of the landscape,
    broad and still;
Or, drifting in the valley with the softly purling
    stream,
To flood the wells of fancy with the sweet,
    transcendent dream
That permeates the atmosphere and, in the
    forest, weaves
Its themes amid the tangle of the variegated leaves.

The charms of budding spring-time and of sum-
      mer's growing field
Are shallow when compared with those these
    , halcyon hours yield;
The undertone of insect life that murmurs, half
      subdued,
Beguiles the wordly soul into an introspective
      mood,
And teaches, by comparison, the better part of life—
The peace of resignation coming after toil and strife,
Whence man's ambitious spirit learns its longings
      to appease,
That earth's divinest music oft is pitched in
      minor keys.

A PICTURE.

'TIS dusk on the river; the dews, softly falling,
    Are decking the tree-tops with sparkles of
      light.   .
From out the low willows the throstle is calling
    And plaintively singing her song to the night.
Among the tall maples the whippoorwill's chiding
    Vociferous frogs that are croaking below,
While slyly the night-hawk comes forth from her
      hiding
    And startles the bats as they flit to and fro.

Far over the river the moonlight is gleaming,
    Reflecting the forms of the shadowy grove,
With all the bright stars, so benignantly beaming
    From out their blue depths in the heavens above;
While down by the water a poet sits dreaming,
    And weaves a fair song for the maid of his love.

A PLAINT OF THE ANCIENT GREEK.

OH, for some Hyperborean strand!
    Some favored Æthiopian shore;
Where, by soft Halcyon breezes fanned,
    The soul might rest forevermore!
Where Pan, the shepherd, herds his flock
    And sweetly play the Æolian lutes,
And Venus, sitting on the rocks,
    Lends Love's sweet charm to all pursuits.

Where soft Apollo blows his horn,
    The Muses charm each soul to rest,
From when Aurora wakes the morn,
    Till Vesper settles in the West;
Where Jupiter his lightnings saves,
    And Hera reigns in full control;
While gay, on Neptune's charmed waves,
    The sea-nymphs gambol as they roll.

Where, all unknown the field of Mars—
    Save when Diana roams the gorge,
And all the household gods of Lars
    Do light their fires at Vulcan's forge.
Where Bacchus brews his foaming bowl—
    The Graces, with their finer arts,
Subdue the Vampires of the soul,
    And Momus rules each joyous heart.

There would I sit in Herme's halls,
    And learn Minerva's golden lore;
Unheeding Fate's incessant squalls
    That vex us on this troubled shore.
O, Emerald Isle beyond the seas!
    I, weary on life's dismal strand,
Am waiting for the gods' decrees
    To call me to that happy land!

THE POET AND HIS SONG.

"WHEN will the poet's song be done?"
    As well ask of the setting sun
When it behind the Western hills
    Will sink to rise no more.
"But will not time exhaust his dream,
    And leave him but a threadbare theme
Of which some earlier Homer's quill
    Has written long before?"

Didst ever hear the robin sing,
Or watch the throstle on the wing,
Or mark the summer storm-cloud roll
    Athwart the welkin blue?
Didst ever walk the beach along
And listen to the ocean's song
But that its echoes thrilled thy soul
    With something strange and new?

Didst ever walk the city street
And mark each face you chanced to meet,
Look on each cot and temple door
    Along the thoroughfare?
Hast ever trod a rural way
Where you have wandered many a day,
Nor marked new objects which, before,
    You never noted there?

So is it with the poet's lay:
He sees beyond the dark array
Of toil and troubles, doubts and fears,
    That vex the common mind;
With knowledge gained through higher art,
He finds the key to every heart,
And strives for all life's bitter tears
    Some soothing balm to find.

Through every nook of Nature's soul
The Muse is given leave to stroll,
And pluck each fragrant flower of thought
    That blossoms 'mid the thorn;
And every flow'ret, fair or frail,
She weaves into a tender tale
Whereby some new-born truth is taught
    Life's temple to adorn.

For those who in the eager quest
Of wealth, find never time to rest,
Save now and then a casual glance
    Upon the printed page;
The poet's many-tinted leaves
Are gathered, though he oft receives
But little praise, till he, perchance,
    Hath found a higher stage.

But, long as Nature's tireless hand
Brings forth her lessons new and grand,
And any of the wordly throng .
    Find pleasure in the dream—
While earth is fair and women pure,
While sun and moon and stars endure,
The poet still will sing his song
    And never lack a theme.

APPENDIX.

NOTE I.—The region along the shores on both sides of the Mississippi between the points of the confluence of the Illinois and Missouri rivers with the Father of Waters, is particularly rich in legendary stories concerning the life and habits of the powerful tribes of Indians who were the original owners of these fertile valley lands. Along the bluffs on the Illinois side are numberless burial places where the bones of thousands of "the first Americans" repose, while the valleys and prairie-stretches for some distance back from the river afford constant reminders of their presence and handiwork in the dim ages of the past. From the time of the earliest frontier expeditions, this locality has been conspicuous among the chronicles for the number and peculiar charm of the folk-lore stories handed down from one generation to another, and held in almost sacred reverence by the Indians. And among these, dating from the famous expedition of Marquette, none is more striking and interesting than that of the Piasa Bird. That this was more than a mere myth is attested by the evidence of many early settlers who got the story in minute detail from the Indians themselves, and by the painting that remained upon the face of the perpendicular bluffs within the present limits of the city of Alton, until quarried away just about the close of the first half of the present century. The picture that forms the frontispiece of this book is from a painting from the original made by Mr. John B. Blair, an artist of genius and renown, who died in Chicago, in December, 1895. It is now owned by Prof. E. Marsh, of this city. The story is fully told in the poem.

NOTE II.—Next to that of the Piasa Bird, the legend of Lover's Leap is perhaps the most noted and interesting of any that cluster around the vicinity of Alton, Ill., but this is the first time that it has ever appeared in written form. The point described is located at the southern-

168

most extremity of Prospect street, in the city of Alton, where it ends in a sheer bluff rising two hundred feet from the bank of the river. It is one of the few landmarks of special interest in this vicinity that have escaped the defacing hand of civilization, and commands one of the most magnificent views to be found anywhere in the Mississippi valley.

NOTE III.—The history of heroism in all ages and among all nations of the globe furnishes few instances of such magnanimous self-sacrifice as that of this savage of the American forests, and the story of his deed does not coincide very well with the oft-repeated and much-credited statement that the Indian possesses no sense of honor, and is incapable of any of the finer traits of character commonly attributed to the people of every other race and nation. There has been some dispute as to his age, and at least one commentator claims that he was very young, instead of a man well advanced in years, when he made himself immortal; but the writer, having examined all evidence obtainable, is satisfied that he has given a true and exact rendition of the legend.

NOTE IV.—The topographical peculiarity that forms the foundation for this poem is indeed most remarkable, and the legend connected therewith is about the most positive of any of the relative themes treated in this book. There can be no question that the story is true, and the old French village of Portage des Sioux, located on the west bank of the Mississippi, in St. Charles county, Mo., bears to-day many unmistakable evidences of early inhabitance by the Indians. A series of mounds within its confines have yielded to the delver's spade some of the richest specimens of aboriginal pottery and implements of war ever unearthed in this country.

NOTE V.—One of the most beautiful effects which the diversity of nature along the limestone bluffs, facing the river in Jersey county, Illinois, affords, is presented in the valley four miles below the mouth of the Illinois river where the Piasa Bluffs Assembly holds its annual summer meetings. This corporation was formed about twelve years ago for the purpose of religious worship and general culture away from city life during the pleasant summer months, by a company of fervent workers in the Methodist Episcopal Church. The natural adaptability of the locality to the purpose has made it an unqualified success from the first, and the improvements made have robbed it of none of its original charm.

169

The spring, which is its greatest glory, possesses some fine medicinal properties, and this fact, together with the surroundings, naturally suggests the legend.

NOTE VI.—A legend of the Miami tribes of the Indiana plains, and true according to the best evidence bearing upon the subject that the author has been able to obtain.

NOTE VII.—This story is oft told and passes current for historical fact among the old scouts, trappers and hunters of the Wisconsin and Michigan woods, who got it direct from the Chippewa Indians, to which tribe it is credited.

NOTE VIII.—This poem was occasioned by one of the saddest episodes ever recorded in the biographical history of Illinois. On Thursday, April 11th, 1895, Prof. Wm. McAdams, accompanied only by his pointer dog, Cleopatra, set sail from Alton up the Mississippi for the inlet to Prairie Lake, on the Missouri shore, fifteen miles above, where a number of friends constituting the Pottawatomie Club, was encamped, enjoying a week's snipe shoot. His failure to arrive on Thursday night occasioned no alarm, as it was supposed that he had stopped at Portage des Sioux to delve in the Indian mounds there. But when, on Friday, his empty boat was found at Clifton, four miles above Alton, adrift, his friends apprehended the worst; and at once started a determined search which was headed by the Professor's sons, Clark and John, and was continued until Sunday afternoon, when the dog was found on a barren sandbar at the foot of Eagle's Nest Island, guarding a little bundle of personal effects. There was the mark of a boat's prow on the sand, and the Professor's tracks where he had stepped ashore, deposited his bundle, and returned to the water. That was all, but it was at once inferred that he had intended to spend the night on the island; that in stepping from the boat he had so lightened it as to cause it to float out from shore, that he had followed incautiously, and gone over a reef. This supposition was confirmed on the following day, when his body, full clothed, was found with grappling lines in twelve feet of water a few yards out. His watch had stopped at 9:15 p. m., and so it was deducted that he went down to his fate at just 9 o'clock, on the night of April 11. The fact that he had spent his life largely in archæological and geological research along the Mississippi, and that he lost his life while upon a pleasure trip to join the Pottawatomie Club, of which he was President, led to the writing of this poem and its dedication to him by the club. Prof. McAdams was one of the most eminent scientists who have honored his profession in this country. He had charge of the Missouri geological display at the New Orleans World's Fair, and of the Illinois display at the Columbian Exposition, was Fellow of the Missouri and and National Academies of Science, and President of the Illinois Society of Natural History, and contributed more than any other man to the literature, of the sciences of geology, archæology and anthropology, as pertaining to the Mississippi Valley. His remains repose in the family cemetery, at the old homestead, near Otterville, in Jersey County, Ill.

NOTE IX.—The landmark herein described is located on a prominent point of the Illinois bluffs, not many miles below Hamburg Bay, and is an object of wonderment of curious inquiry to all travelers up and down the Upper Mississippi.

NOTE X.—The biographers of President Lincoln and General Shields have generally omitted to mention the fact of this sanguinary encounter between these two eminent Illinoisans, in the days of their youthful ardor, but the episode is nevertheless historically correct as here narrated, and there are some men yet living in the State who have a personal recollection of the incident. The Island in the Mississippi river, near Alton, Ill., where the duelists met, is still pointed out to inquiring strangers.

NOTE XI.—Written on the occasion of the first opening of the World's Columbian Exposition, at Chicago, in celebration of the 400th anniversary of the sailing of Columbus, upon the voyage which resulted in the discovery of America.

NOTE XII.—This poem is a translation from the German of Mrs. Marie Raible, of this city. It is given as an example of many poems that the author has had the privilege of translating for Mrs. Raible, whose friendship he is proud to possess, and who is recognized as the second greatest writer of German poetry now living in America. The two succeeding poems are taken from among many translations from various German authors.

171

NOTE XIII.—There is an old legend among the Germans of a fair island city situated somewhere near the mouth of the Rhine, which, one night, during a severe storm, disappeared beneath the waves. Now a magic light illumes the waters where the island went down, and often as the sun sinks beneath the western hills the mermaids in those submarine halls toll the bells in the old church towers of the submerged city; and he who once sees this light and hears the solemn dirge of the bells is irresistibly drawn towards the spot, until the waves sweep over him and he sinks to the bottom.

GENERAL NOTE.—The writer deems it his duty, as well as a pleasant privilege, to state, in conclusion of these comments, that while some of the poems herein published are printed for the first time, and many have been re-written and improved, he owes his introducton to the general public to the occasional appearance of much of his work in the Alton "Telegraph," "Sentinel-Democrat" and "Daily Republican," and to such magazines as "Home and Country," "Blue and Gray," "Outing," "The American Angler," "The Waterways Journal," "The National Journalist" and "The American Journal of Education."

www.ingramcontent.com/pod-product-compliance
Lightning Source LLC
Chambersburg PA
CBHW020227030726
47497CB00009B/2985